THE LONESOME GUN

It's a fateful day for Orde Clemmins, foreman of the Star and Bar Ranch. A mysterious stranger — the spitting image of Luke Strang — is driving cattle onto his land. But hadn't Clemmins and his men chased Strang to Skeleton Desert and certain death . . . ? In fact, Luke Strang's son, Rod has returned to Arizona to claim his inheritance. But the odds are heavily stacked against him — a bloody shoot-out means many men will die before justice is done.

KEN BROMPTON

THE LONESOME GUN

Complete and Unabridged

LINFORD
Leicester

First published in Great Britain in 2001

Originally published in paperback as
The Lonesome Gun by A. A. Glynn

First Linford Edition
published 2010

The moral right of the author has been asserted

British Library CIP Data

Brompton, Ken, *1929* –
  The lonesome gun.- -
  (Lindord western library)
  1. Western stories.
  2. Large type books.
  I. Title II. Series III. Glynn, A. A.
  823.9'14–dc22

  ISBN 978–1–44480–127–9

Published by
F. A. Thorpe (Publishing)
Anstey, Leicestershire

Set by Words & Graphics Ltd.
Anstey, Leicestershire
Printed and bound in Great Britain by
T. J. International Ltd., Padstow, Cornwall

1

Orde Clemmins, foreman of the Star and Bar, was quenching his thirst with cool beer in Joe Bannock's saloon when the two strangers and the couple of dozen head of trail-wearied cattle came stirring up sun-sparkled columns of dust out on San Junipero's single street.

Clemmins was half leaning across the scuffed oak of the bar, his Peacemaker Colt looking conspicuous at his hip. He liked it to look that way; it was a sort of badge of office, marking him as fore-man of a tough cow-outfit. He'd held down that job at the Star and Bar for nearly twenty years — ever since Colo-nel Cal Tedrow came to Arizona licking his war wounds, grabbed himself part of the big country and built himself a cattle empire, manned by Texans who rode with him against the Yankees.

The burly foreman of the Star and

Bar was engaged in conversation with Charlie Curry, another veteran Star and Bar rider. He paused after a sentence, raised his schooner of beer to his lips — then, through the big window of the saloon, saw the men and cattle out on the street. Orde Clemmins placed the vessel back on the bar without taking any of its contents. His eyes, with their deep-etched fringes of crow's feet wrinkles, were round as dimes, peering fixedly through the dust-grimed glass of the saloon window at the two men on cow-ponies escorting the straggle of dusty beef-on-the-hoof.

'It can't be!' he murmured to himself, a strange huskiness edging his voice. 'It just *can't* be!'

'What ails you, Orde?' demanded Curry. 'You look like a fellow that's seen a ghost!'

'Ain't so sure I ain't seen a ghost!' husked Clemmins. 'One of them two *hombres* who just passed the window with them cows — he was the spittin' image of Luke Strang!'

* ★ *

Charlie Curry jumped visibly and switched his gaze to the window. He saw the straggle of longhorns moving up the centre of the hoof-mauled street through a fog of dust hanging on the drowsy air. The two men were, by this time, only a pair of vague mounted shapes up at the head of the column of beef. Curry could see only their backs through the obscuring banners of dust.

'You're crazy, Orde. Luke Strang is dead,' he told his companion. 'He died twelve years ago when we chased him out on Skeleton Desert.'

'We didn't find his body,' stated Clemmins, still staring fixedly through the saloon window.

'We found his bones! They must have been *his* bones! Come to think of it, who are those *hombres* drivin' cattle through this town? There's only one cow-outfit on these ranges.'

The expression of stunned fear dissolved from Orde Clemmins's blocky

3

face and was replaced by a tight-lipped scowl of determination. He thumped his Peacemaker loose in its leather.

'You're right, Charlie. An' only one outfit is stayin' on these ranges. Let's take a look at these rannihans.'

They strode for the door, Clemmins tall and solidly built, nearing fifty years of age and Curry shorter and wiry, a couple of years younger than the foreman of the Star and Bar.

They crossed the scarred boardwalk, emerged from the shadow of the warped awning into the full blaze of the desert sun on the hoof-pitted and animal-fouled width of San Junipero's street, The tail end of the couple of dozen head of cattle was moving past them now. Little knots of people stood at intervals along the boardwalks, watching the progress of the small herd and Clemmins and Curry saw that it was the unknown brand burned into the flanks of the slatty beeves that held their attention.

The only cattle the people of San Junipero were accustomed to seeing

4

moving through their town was Star and Bar stock. Star and Bar was the only big cow-outfit hereabouts, San Junipero receiving most of its verve from booming silver and copper mines. But the trail-lean longhorns that now churned up the gritty dust of Main Street were burned with an iron alien to the San Junipero vicinity.

It was a Running S.

'I don't get this,' observed Charlie Curry. 'I never saw that iron in my life. They can't be drivin' those cows to Star and Bar; we ain't done business with anybody, have we, Orde?'

'No, we ain't bought stock from anybody,' grunted the foreman. 'We ain't bought any beef from anyone ownin' that brand or any other. This looks plumb funny. Those critters are bein' herded out towards our rangers!'

At that instant, the taller of the two riders escorting the cattle, a ghostly figure in the hazing dust upstreet, yanked his lean body around in the saddle, spotted a half-grown animal straggling out of the line of jostling horns, hauled his pony about and rode back down the herd to scare the rebel back where she belonged. As he moved through the swirls of dust, his features became clearer to Clemmins and Curry. The Star and Bar men felt washes of eerie fear seeping in waves down their backbones.

Under the warped brim of his sombrero, the stranger's face was that of Luke Strang — Luke Strang whom Star and Bar riders had hounded to certain death on Skeleton Desert, south of this town, a dozen years before!

The tall rider's features were lean and high-cheekboned. Straggles of sweat plastered hair escaped from under his hat and clung to his broad forehead. His nose was straight and high bridged and there was glitter to his steel grey eyes that marked him as a man dedicated to something. He wore a Colt .45 slung low and strapped hard against his thigh — worn as though it was part of him.

Clemmins and Curry watched the rider with their feelings of awe on the increase. Where Luke Strang had been somewhere in his thirties when they chased him off Star and Bar ranges twelve years earlier, this man could only be in his middle twenties, but his face was that of Luke Strang.

The rider chased the straggler back into the herd and, partly to release himself from the tension of nervous awe, Orde Clemmins suddenly yelled: 'Hey there, *hombre!* Where are you takin' that beef?'

The cry brought the horseman's attention to the Star and Bar men for the first time.

He saw the bulky figure of Clemmins, his gun looking big and obtrusive, and the smaller form of Curry. Both held truculent poses in the centre of the street.

Something like a smile quirked the corners of the stranger's mouth upwards, but it was a smile without humour. He twisted his head around and called over his shoulder.

7

'Keep 'em movin' on yore own, Nacio!'

Then he touched spur barbs to his pony and jounced down the sun-punished street with jingling ringbits, yanking his rein when he reached the men from Star and Bar. Arrogance was stamped on his weather-stained face.

Causing Orde Clemmins to jump visibly, the stranger said:

'So, it's Clemmins, the foreman of Colonel Tedrow's spread! Were you addressin' yoreself to me, Clemmins?'

Clemmins felt the flood of fear washing over him. He was on the edge of something beyond his experience.

This stranger knew his name. This man who had Luke Strang's face.

But he couldn't be Luke Strang, insisted a portion of the foreman's mind. He had himself seen the bundle of bleached, buzzard-cleaned bones generally accepted to be those of Strang. Furthermore, Strang couldn't be this young, even if he were still alive.

Utterly confused and frightened,

Clemmins took refuge in his customary loud-mouthed bluster.

'I was addressin' myself to you, Mister! Where are you takin' those cows? Who are you, anyway?'

Without taking his gaze from the foreman's face, the man in the saddle jerked a thumb towards a line of high land, shrouded in heat-haze to the north of town.

'See those pastures out there? That's where I'm takin' these cows. Yore outfit's goin' to have a new neighbour, Clemmins, the Runnin' S. I'm goin' up there to start a cow-outfit,' he declared with calculated insolence in every lazily pronounced word. 'As for who I am, I figure you'll find out soon enough.'

Orde Clemmins opened and closed his mouth a couple of times without any words coming, but Charlie Curry found his voice.

'You can't run cattle up there!' he gasped, as though the stranger had uttered some terrible blasphemy in suggesting it. 'That's Star and Bar land!'

9

'Yeah,' joined in Clemmins. 'That's Star and Bar land. Nobody is goin' to run another brand on that pasture!'

The mirthless smile lifted the corners of the mounted man's mouth again.

'Is that so?' he murmured. 'Can either of you two tell me who's goin' to stop me?'

'We are!' snarled Clemmins, finding his old brash spirit. 'The whole Star and Bar outfit!'

To Orde Clemmins, Charlie Curry and the rest of the original Star and Bar riders, their outfit was the most important thing in the world. They were devoted to it with the fervour of zealots. In a way, Star and Bar was a continuation of the lost cause for which they had fought twenty years before when they wore Rebel grey and rode with Lee.

When the South was defeated, Clemmins and Curry were two of the hard riding Texas cavalrymen who stayed with their old colonel, hit the Arizona trail to mould a cattle empire out of the untamed land. They had to lick Apaches to do it and they accomplished this by riding against the desert warriors with all the fury they had unleashed at the blue-clad Yankees.

From the emblems on the old Confederate States' battle flag — the 'Stars and Bars' — they fashioned a brand and stamped that iron hard upon the land in the San Junipero vicinity. Building up the Star and Bar spread was a way of working off their soreness at being licked by Lincoln's Federals.

In the early days, Colonel Cal Tedrow would ride with his range crews wearing his old Rebel officer's coat with the 'chicken guts' — the yellow piping marking his rank — still worked proudly on the sleeves. When Star and Bar men chased snorty steers or gathered a herd, they whooped the old 'Rebel yell', the throaty screech that was entirely the property of the Confederate soldier and which had put the fear of the Last Judgment into the Yankees who heard it voiced from advancing waves of grey at Shilo, Antietam and Gettysburg.

All the stubbornness of the Old South was in the Star and Bar outfit, and the ranch's hard fought for heritage prodded Orde Clemmins to action as he faced this insolent young stranger who calmly declared the intention of putting his trail-gaunt cows on Star and Bar grass. The foreman shook his fist at the mounted man.

'We'll stop you!' he mouthed excitedly. 'We'll stop you before you even have a chance to get started! By grab, I have a mind to push yore nose clear through to the back of yore head, Mister!'

'You talk too much, Clemmins,' answered the stranger, with his icy smile. 'You're wastin' my time an' I have a herd to move.'

'Come down from that cayuse, by cracky, an' I'll deal with you!' bellowed the enraged foreman.

'An' I'll help him,' added Charlie Curry who was holding down his hot anger better than Clemmins.

By this time, a sizeable group of people had gathered to watch the altercation in the middle of the street; they were mostly men in stained miners' garb, one or two women in sunbonnets and a scattering of Mexicans and Indians. This audience saw the tall stranger swing down from his battered El Paso saddle with easy grace. At his back, away up the street, the straggle of cattle and its accompanying cloud of dust was growing smaller as the tall man's companion herded them upstreet, heading for that range of hilly pastureland north of San Junipero's clutter of timber and adobe structures.

With an almost lazy stride, the tall man came level with Clemmins and Curry.

'You won't deal with anybody, Clemmins,' he stated flatly.

Then, with amazing rapidity, he swept his right hand upwards, placed it flat in the middle of the foreman's face with the fingers outspread and shoved with all his might.

Orde Clemmins, looking like a clown in a circus ring, did a crazy little dance as he teetered backwards off balance. Then, he sat down in the dirt as abruptly as if his legs had been swept from under him.

A titter of mirth rippled through the knot of watching people. There was a breathless snarl from Charlie Curry and he clawed for the butt of his Colt.

The moment the Star and Bar man moved, the tall stranger twisted his lean body slightly to face him and, even as he moved, the .45 seemed to leap out of his lowriding holster into his hand. Charlie Curry found himself at the loser's end of the fastest draw he'd ever seen in his life.

Chilled by fear, he stared at the blue steel of the gun which covered him unwaveringly. His fingers had not even reached the butt of his own weapon.

'Stand still,' purred the stranger. 'An' you down there, Clemmins, don't entertain any notions about pullin' yore iron. I'd drop you before you even commenced!'

Clemmins was gathering himself up. One portion of his mind had been calculating whether he could slap leather and yank his six-gun while the stranger's attention was diverted by Curry. He now abandoned that scheme. This stranger, this enigma with the features of a man who was supposed to be dead, not only had the fastest gun hand ever seen in San Junipero, he also seemed to possess the gift of mind reading.

The Star and Bar foreman came to his feet slowly shaking his head to clear tears started by the violent push of the stranger's hand in his face. He grunted and snorted with humiliated indignation. Both Clemmins and Curry stood quite still, looking like chastized children.

With a languid movement, the young stranger dropped his six-shooter back into its holster.

'You two had better be about yore business,' he advised. 'An', when you get back to Star and Bar headquarters, you can tell yore boss I'm puttin' beef on those northern ranges. I'm buildin' a house up there, too. Star and Bar has had it too easy hereabouts for too many years. You have a neighbour now, like it or not!'

Clemmins and Curry glowered and muttered under their breath as they moved for the hitch-rack outside Joe Bannock's saloon. They were too humiliated and confused to return to the saloon to finish the schooners of beer they had left scarcely tasted. In the last few minutes, things had happened to up-end their whole world.

The advent of the man with Luke Strang's face had brought trouble that would not end with Orde Clemmins being pushed on his rear in the centre of Main Street and Charlie Curry being made to look a fool when he grabbed for his gun. This was something they knew too well and it called for consultations at Star and Bar headquarters.

Clemmins and Curry forked their

broncs and rode out of town, turning their heads frequently to bestow dark glances on the stranger as they went.

The stranger was about to climb back to his saddle when a short, flashily dressed man detached himself from the little cluster of townsfolk who had watched the humiliation of Clemmins and Curry. He wore a neat broadcloth suit, a loudly checkered cravat in which a large diamond pin glittered and a grey beaver hat. Under the jauntily tilted brim of the beaver, the man's face was broad and bland. His nose was short and somewhat bulbous; his mouth was wide with fleshy lips; his eyes were small and too near together. There were flecks of grey in the sandy sideburns that were combed neatly down from his ears almost to chin level. The flashily dressed one was in his late forties and his air of prosperity was akin to that of a lucky Mississippi steamboat gambler.

'Congratulations, friend,' he said to the stranger. 'That Star and Bar foreman had a shove in the face coming to him for a long time. Always was a blusterer. One hard blow is all it usually takes to deflate his kind.'

The stranger hooked a cracked boot into a stirrup and hoisted his spare frame into his saddle.

'Why didn't someone give him what he needed before now?' he enquired lazily.

'Nobody had the guts, I guess.' responded the prosperous looking one. 'That's the trouble around here; nobody ever had the guts to pull Star and Bar down to size.' He dropped his voice to a confidential tone and added:

'As a matter of fact, young fellow, pulling Star and Bar down is a proposition I'm mighty interested in myself and I gather that's a scheme that appeals to you. I heard what you said to Clemmins and I saw the way you pulled that gun — never seen a draw like it! Seems to me, Mister, that you're a man I could use . . . '

'Nothin' doin',' cut in the stranger crisply.

'Now, wait a moment, friend. You haven't heard me out . . . '

'Nothin' doin',' stated the mounted man abruptly. He was fixing the other with a stony stare, a stare that bespoke the fact this man was not one to argue with. 'I don't know you, Mister, an' I don't want to know you. I'm not interested in any of yore schemes. Furthermore, I'm nobody's man but my own so, if yore lookin' for a man you can use, don't come to me!'

He yanked his rein and thumped his knees into his cow-pony's ribs, urging the mount forward at a smart trot in the direction of the flats north of town which his companion and the herd had already reached.

The flashily dressed one stood in the middle of the street watching the back of the riding man for a long time and rubbing his smooth chin thoughtfully. His eyes held a hard glow.

'He doesn't like Star and Bar and he doesn't like me,' he growled to himself. 'Who'd have figured on this kind of dog in the manger showing up at a time like this? I'll have to get rid of him pretty darn quick, somehow!'

2

It was night, the scented night of early summer in Arizona. After the blaze of day, the air had a soft and pleasantly warm caress.

Rod Strang stretched himself contentedly against a rock slab and rolled a smoke. In the background, the two cowponies were munching on the good grass of these high pastures. Down on the flats, points of yellow light marked the situation of San Junipero.

The blaze of the campfire on which a blackened coffee pot bubbled painted bright highlights on the gaunt features of Rod Strang and on the dark, moustache-embellished face of Ignacio Laca.

Ignacio was relishing a thin Mexican cigarillo, his bulky form stretched out before the fire and his ornately tooled Spanish saddle serving as a pillow for his bald head. Laca was fifteen years older than Rod Strang, which made him thirty-nine. They were partners and their partnership began years before, south of the border. Together, they had followed their fortunes in many parts of the western frontier. They'd herded half-frozen cows, knee-deep in the snow that came swirling across the Montana ranges on the howling wind out of Canada. They'd helped prod a fractious sea of cattle clear from Texas to Dodge City; they'd grubbed after gold in a shortlived and quite phoney 'strike' in Nebraska, found only rocks and worms and laughed about it and they'd held down the jobs of marshal and deputy in a savage Dakota town. Whatever they did, they did together.

Now, they had embarked on a scheme which had been in Rod Strang's mind for years. They came to Arizona to make trouble for the Star and Bar spread and to build themselves a ranch.

And they were going to do it together.

Ignacio Laca blew a thin stream of smoke up towards the desert stars.

'A pretty good day, Rod,' he observed in English which bore only a slight trace of Mexican accent. 'A pretty good day all round.'

'Yeah, Nacio, I guess we can say we dug our heels into this land.'

They settled themselves into the silent enjoyment of their smokes, waiting for the second brew of after-dinner coffee to heat up. They'd enjoyed a dinner of canned pork and beans and, before the meal, had put in three sweating hours building a brush pen for the herd. They had the cattle penned in it by sundown. Now, they could allow their meal to digest, smoke, rest their bones and contemplate.

Ignacio closed his eyes, his round features reposing into a picture of contentment while Rod thought of what he'd make of this stretch of pasturage. Some distance from this point, where flat rocks made a natural hearth for their camp-fire, there was a

23

good spot on which a house could be built. There were a couple of timber stands nearby from which wood for the building and barns could be cut.

Two or three months' work here, and a tolerably smart little ranch would be shaping up, thought Rod, grinding out his spent cigarette on the sole of his boot. That would be something to make old Colonel Tedrow and his riders get mad and snorty.

Not that it would work out that easy, of course. There was going to be plenty of trouble before he got halfway to building his Running S headquarters. But they'd take them on; Rod Strang and Nacio Laca against the whole Star and Bar.

And they'd lick Tedrow's crew of wild Texans.

Wild Texans! That was how Rod Strang had always thought of Colonel Tedrows' riders. He'd thought of them that way ever since a night fourteen years before.

He was twelve then, living with his

24

father in the little homesteader shack close to the fringe of Star and Bar grass. Luke Strang settled on the land under the Homesteader Act. He had every right to be there, but Colonel Tedrow and his Star and Bar crew thought otherwise.

They objected to him mostly because he was a Yankee. The story that he'd been with Sherman's ruthless columns when they made their pillaging march through Georgia got around among the erstwhile Confederates of Star and Bar. As it happened, this was not true. Luke Strang had served as a sergeant with Grant until Rebel fire crippled his right hand in the Vicksburg campaign.

But the myth was good enough for the Star and Bar hotheads. He was a Yankee who'd marched through the Southland with Sherman. He'd done his share of plantation-burning and robbery. He'd heaped indignities on noble Southern womanhood while its menfolk were away at the war. Even if there had been someone to tell the Star and Bar riders the truth, they wouldn't have been interested.

They wouldn't have been interested in the fact that Sergeant Luke Strang was as good a soldier and as fair a fighter as they could wish to encounter. They wouldn't have cared that he had once given the last of his own personal rations to a Rebel widow and her family after fleeing Rebels had divested her little Virginia farm of every last morsel of food. It wouldn't have mattered to them that he'd written a letter home for many a wounded enemy prisoner or that he'd once whaled the living daylights out of a light-fingered Yankee corporal whom he'd caught robbing Southern prisoners of their few valuables.

Luke Strang was a pillaging Yankee who'd rode with Sherman, and he was building himself a homestead on the land for which Star and Bar had licked Apaches. That was the myth which was retailed among Tedrow's men in their bunkhouse and it was good enough for them.

Widower Strang worked hard at building up his nester's plot into something worthwhile. Manual work was difficult for him because of his crippled hand, but he tackled it with a stolid determination and achieved results slowly. His wife had died three years before and it was her death which decided him to pull up stakes from the little Ohio farm his father had bequeathed him and try his luck in the Southwest. So, he came to the edge of Star and Bar's ranges — which was public land, no matter what Tedrow and his Texans claimed.

Tedrow and his Texans did not interfere with the nester and his small son for the first eight months, but that was the formulative period of the myth. While Luke Strang was struggling through his first Arizona winter, Star and Bar riders were telling it around the bunkhouse stove that that Yankee down yonder on the edge of the south pasture had been one of old Sherman's 'bummers'.

Through the winter, the myth grew.

In the spring, Star and Bar made its first raid.

It was April and Luke Strang had just put in his first sowing of corn. To be exact, it was April 12th, the anniversary of the South's first blow for what it termed 'states' rights'. On that day in 1861, General Beauregard's cannon had opened up on Yankee-manned Fort Sumter in Charleston Bay. The anniversary afforded an excuse for a drinking spree and bushy-bearded Tedrow, who could be as wildly boisterous as any of his riders, took them off to San Junipero.

The whiskey had them plenty excited when someone yipped:

'Why don't we go an' give that Yankee nester a whippin? We don't want none of Sherman's brigands on our land, do we? Why don't we ride over an' show him Star and Bar land ain't healthy for his kind?'

In their high-flying state of intoxication, the Star and Bar men — the owner of the ranch included — found this a suggestion to be acted upon.

They came to Luke Strang's homestead plot when the sun was dying redly in the wide skies to the west. It streaked the thundering riders with a glow of crimson as they came down the slope of the land off Star and Bar grass, making them look like demon horsemen emerging from the gates of hell. As they came, they whooped Rebel yells.

Luke Strang told his son to stay inside the cabin, opened the door and stood there, waiting for them.

Rod never forgot the way his father stood there, completely composed and strangely dignified in his grubby jeans and torn shirt.

The boy stood at the small window at one side of the door. He watched the screaming, wide-hatted demons come riding their stretched out mounts towards the cabin while his heart pounded madly. He knew his father didn't own a gun. Rod knew, too, that his father couldn't handle a gun even if he had owned one; his gun-handling days finished when Confederate fire shattered his right hand. When his hand healed into a twisted thing, Luke Strang had learned to handle many things well with his left hand, but not guns. So far as he was concerned, guns belonged in the war and the war was over.

The Star and Bar men yanked their reins in front of the small cabin and sat their saddles, grinning wolfishly at the man who stood at the door. Colonel Tedrow was at their head, a big man in a floppy brimmed hat. The small boy watching from the window never forgot the rancher's handsome features and the way the setting sun put an outline of crimson to his full beard.

Like his men, Cal Tedrow was drunk. whooping drunk.

'Yankee,' he roared, 'we've come over here to show you this ain't no place for dirt-scratchin' nesters — least of all yore kind. This is Star and Bar land an' we aim to keep it. We propose to give you somethin' that'll make you think it's preferable to run for yore life!'

'Ain't much I can do about that, I guess,' answered Luke Strang evenly. 'But this ain't Star and Bar grass and you know it. I settled here legally under the Homestead Act.'

'Homestead Act!' Colonel Tedrow spat out the words. 'Yankee acts don't carry much weight hereabouts, Strang. This is a long ways from Washington an' we ain't got much time for the Washington government. All we got time for is our right to the land we whipped Apaches for!'

Luke Strang sighed. This was the sort of talk he'd heard time and again when he went into San Junipero for supplies. Star and Bar men who happened to be in town would make this kind of talk, taking care he would overhear them. During the war, Arizona was strongly pro-Confederate and Luke Strang soon learned that old loyalties lingered long and he was a man among enemies.

'Just because you fought the Indians for the land don't mean you own all of Arizona, Colonel,' he told the owner of

Star and Bar. 'Other people have a right to live, too.'

'Not on this land!' thundered Tedrow. 'Not blasted, plunderin', burnin', blue-bellied Yankees that marched with Sherman. I'm through with talkin' — commence, you *hombres!*'

They commenced.

Systematically, they trampled their horses over the patch Luke Strang had lately sowed. They went around the back of the cabin and shot the milk cow. They burned the small outhouse in which the homesteader kept his equipment. They rode around the cabin in a Rebel-yelling bunch, shooting their six-guns at random so that Luke Strang and his son had to lie on the floor of the dwelling as bullets shattered the small window and whanged around inside the cabin.

Presently, they had their fill and they bunched up in a triumphant group in front of the cabin door. Luke Strang still had the nerve to open the door and face them. He was shaken. His face was strangely altered, haggard and drawn. In a few minutes, these men had ruined the work of months.

'That's only a taste, Yankee,' shouted Tedrow. 'You stick around here much longer an' there'll be plenty worse to come! If you take my advice, you'll take off from these parts, *muy pronto!*'

Rod Strang remembered the way his father had stood motionless in the doorway, watching the grinning cowhands yank their mounts around to ride for home. Luke Strang held his peace for a moment, then he thundered in a voice that seemed not to be his own, a strong and powerful voice, but one that seemed to waver on the brink of a sob:

'I'm staying, Tedrow! You won't chase me out, you'll have to kill me! And I hope you're proud of yourself for this night's work! I hope *you're* proud of yourself as a Southern officer — because General Lee, or Stonewall Jackson would never be proud of your behaviour, neither would Wade Hampton or Jeb Stuart!'

Young Rod Strang was watching from the bullet-starred window. He saw the effect of these words on the owner of Star and Bar.

The riding party was just beginning to mount the rise which gave on to Star and Bar land proper. At the head of the party, Colonel Cal Tedrow reined his big horse to an abrupt stop as the nester bellowed after him. He pranced the horse around and sat his saddle, motionless, facing the cabin, while the remainder of the party continued up the slope at his back.

The sun was not yet fully down. Its light slanted redly across the wide land and it was possible to see Tedrow's face even at the distance at which he sat his horse from the cabin. The small boy who watched from the window never forgot the expression on the rancher's face as he stared directly at the man standing in the cabin door.

Tedrow's head was slightly lowered and his face thrust forward. The waning light painted the features under the floppy hat with a brush of crimson. The eyes of the old officer's bearded face were round with a penetrating stare. His anger and his wolfish grin were no longer in evidence. Tedrow and Luke Strang held their poses for a full minute, motionless and with eyes locked.

Rod Strang never fathomed the meaning of the expression on the face of the man who watched his father in that long moment. It was the last time he saw Colonel Cal Tedrow and, whenever he thought of him, he thought of him as he looked at that moment.

Slowly, Cal Tedrow turned his horse around and rode up the slope at the rear of his men. There was a distinct droop to his frame as he disappeared into the red-tinted dusk.

The following day, Luke Strang gathered Rod's belongings together and hitched his horse — which Tedrow's raiders had left alive, following their rough western code that a man didn't kill a horse unless he had to, any more than he'd steal one — to his old buckboard. He drove his son to Tucson and there put him on an eastbound train with a letter for his married sister back in Ohio.

Briefly, the letter stated that there were difficulties in Arizona and it would be better for the boy to stay in Ohio and attend school for a spell and his father would send for him when life on the homestead was smoother. Rod knew that his father was going to stay put on the edge of Star and Bar land and make a stand against Tedrow and his crew. He wanted to remain there with his father, but Luke Strang was adamant; he was going to his Aunt Beth in Ohio.

Rod stayed in Ohio for three years. He went to school, learned fast and grew faster. Between times, he helped his Aunt Beth and Uncle Walter around their farm and, all the time, longed to be back in the Southwest, making a stand with his father against those wild Texans.

Texans became something he brooded over. Texans were loud-mouthed braggers. Texans were men who rode around a lone man's small homestead, shooting off guns and whooping. Texans were blusterers and bullies and, some day, he'd stand against Texans with his father and whittle them down to size.

Rod didn't hear from his father for a long time. Often, when he lay in his comfortable room in the Ohio farmhouse, he wondered if Colonel Tedrow's Star and Bar Texans were riding against his father that night. When he looked from the schoolhouse window and saw men working in the fields beyond the white picket fence bordering the dirtroad, he wondered about his father. Maybe his father would be working on the Arizona land, as those men worked on the land of Ohio. Maybe Tedrow's wild Texans would come upon him, drunken and yelling — maybe they'd shoot him dead!

Maybe, he thought with a cold fear when he considered the long intervals between letters, his father was already dead!

But his father was not dead. A letter came one day.

It came from Mexico.

Aunt Beth and Uncle Walter read it with interest. Luke had quit Arizona and was living south of the border. There wasn't much in the way of an explanation as to why he'd given up the homestead. Luke simply said that things had not worked out the way he had expected and he'd found a job with a wealthy Mexican landowner. The landowner wanted an American with capability and a reasonable education to handle some aspects of his business and had apparently found the right man in Luke Strang. The erstwhile Arizona homesteader wanted his son to join him.

So, young Rod Strang travelled to Mexico, to live with his father on the hacienda of Don Ernesto Laca.

Don Ernesto was an aristocrat of the old school. He owned a spacious spread of land in the far south of the state of Chihuahua; he ran large herds of cattle and was notably humane to his peons. The old hidalgo had one son, Ignacio. Ignacio was a shadowy man, a strange, outlaw figure. In Rod Strang's boyhood on the Mexican hacienda, Ignacio showed up only rarely. Then, he came riding with half-a-dozen armed peons accompanying him. He always came at night, a silent horseman in the rough garb of a peon. Ignacio and his companions would stay for perhaps an hour each time. They would eat and drink, stretch their legs and catch brief naps. Ignacio and his men rarely spoke on these visits to the hacienda and when they did speak it was always with Don Ernesto; always cautious and always in whispers were these conversations with the hidalgo.

When the riders left, nobody ever referred to their having visited the Hacienda Laca. From the patrone himself to the poorest peon, lips were sealed.

Luke Strang became Don Ernesto's right hand man and confidant.

'Son,' he told Rod, shortly after the boy arrived from over the border, 'Don Ernesto has done plenty for me and the best way we can repay him is by never mentioning his son and his men and their visits here. There is a good reason for not doing so.'

Rod Strang grew to manhood at the Hacienda Laca, and he harboured his own private notions and dreams. He spent hours in secluded places, brushing up the technique of drawing a Colt .45 from its holster and seeking perfection as a gunhand. Some day, he would need a fast draw — when he went back to Arizona to make a bid against Tedrow's rowdy Texas bunch for the land they ran his father off.

The day of his return to United States territory came with dramatic abruptness. Ignacio came to the hacienda one night. He was alone, weary and wounded and in a desperate hurry to cross the border into Texas. The

40

reasons for Ignacio's shadowy life, which Rod Strang had long suspected, were confirmed as he helped dress the injured man's wounds that night. Ignacio was the leader of a revolutionary band which fought the forces of the tyrant President Porfirio Diaz, once a national hero but now an iron-handed dictator.

For Ignacio, a long run of good luck had broken. He and his dark-of-the-moon riders had harried Diaz's *federale* troops and *rurale* policemen with audacity and courage. But they had finally fallen into a night ambush in the desert-edge region of Chihuahua.

Several bullet-bitten hours of mixing, it with the government troops had ended with all Ignacio's band stretched in death and their leader severely wounded. Almost by a miracle, he had slipped out of the trap under cover of darkness and made a desperate horseback trip north.

At the hacienda, Rod Strang realized that Ignacio was in no shape to make the long trip to the Texas border alone. He offered to ride with the wounded Mexican.

Together, they set out on a journey which opened years of exile for Ignacio Laca and gave Rod his opportunity to begin working for the bid he aimed to make for the land his father had tried to farm on the fringes of Star and Bar grass. Together, they began their years of wandering and saving, each man with his personal dream. Rod's was to even up with the Star and Bar crew and take back the land from which the Texas rannihans had driven his father and Nacio's was to return some day to the land where there was a price on his head to take part in the violent anti-Diaz revolution which, he declared, was bound to come.

Together, they had survived dozens of wild scrapes and Rod saved enough money to buy the beginnings of a cattle herd which he boldly moved on to the good pastureland which Star and Bar claimed as its own. And so, his bold move to pay back his score against Star and Bar commenced. But, for both him and Nacio, the edge had been taken off the move.

Rod had hoped to establish an Arizona ranch — no matter how Star and Bar objected. And he hoped to bring his father back to Arizona Territory from his exile in Mexico. Only a few months before, in New Mexico, the pair had met a Mexican peon who had once worked for Don Ernesto. The peon's news from south of the border was distressing. A smallpox outbreak had taken its toll at the Hacienda Laca. Dozens of peons had died. So had Don Ernesto and his trusted *Americano* assistant, Luke Strang.

The news was a sledgehammer blow to both men. It seemed wholly unfitting and unjust that men of the calibre of Don Ernesto and Luke Strang should come to their end through a mere disease. But that had been the way of it and it strengthened both in their purpose of bucking Star and Bar.

Cocking a snook at the rowdy ex-Confederates down in Arizona gave a solid reason for living to both Luke Strang's son and the son of the Mexican *patrone* who could not claim his father's lands because of the Mexican government's reward on his head.

Thus, they came to the high pastures of the Star and Bar's desert edge ranges. Thus, they built a brush pen for the slatty beeves and settled beside their camp fire.

Thus, they came, also, to the edge of the chasm of death.

3

Rod Strang stirred in the night. He lay in his bedroll at one side of the dying embers of the fire in the rock hearth. Nacio Laca made a humped outline at the other side.

A noise had disturbed Strang's light sleep. Not a natural noise; not the restive jostling of the cattle in the brush pen; not the whisper of the night breeze in the nearby timber but a sound which spoke of the presence of man. A half-heard metallic click.

The sound of a round being pumped into the breach of a repeating carbine!

Strang acted speedily. He pitched his blankets aside, lashing out with a foot to hit the coffee pot close to the fire, sending its cold dregs hissing into the embers to quench their feeble light. As he grabbed for his gun-gear, close to the saddle on which his head had been pillowed, he hissed in sharp alarm:

'Nacio!'

The warning was lost in the flat, far-echoing bellow of a nearby Winchester. A second shot slammed close on the first and the bullet spanged off a rock near to the head of the low-crouching Strang. Rod Strang was fully clothed, but without boots and hat. Clutching his Colt, he rolled across the sandy floor of the rock cluster in which he and his partner had bedded. He slithered snake-like between two rocks, squinting through the darkness in the direction of the upland timber clump from which the shots came. A third shot crashed out of the timber, the slug whining spitefully into the rock cluster. The white bayonet of muzzle-fire, slashing the night, gave Strang a marker as to the position of the bushwhacker and he triggered a couple of shots up at the spot in the timber from which the blaze had flowered. Then, bent double, he hared on a curving course up towards the timber.

46

From the black cluster of the trees, the Winchester rasped again, sending a shot at the position from which Strang had fired. Shambling forward at a crouch, Rod Strang moved up towards the timber stand. Crimson fury blazed in him, goading him onwards so that he did not feel the rough ground under his stockinged feet. There were several yards between the timber and Strang, and he felt reasonably sure that the night was too dark for the man with the Winchester to see him approaching up the rise of the land.

There was silence from the trees. Strang edged forward, trigger-finger tensed, almost praying for the bushwhacker to cut loose with his Winchester again to give him a guide as to his exact position. There was a moment of tension and deadly silence, then a quick rustle in the timber and the brief snort of a horse.

Strang flung himself down to the dark ground, his six-gun bucking, lacing the night with random shots fired in the direction of the noise.

From the trees came the thump of hoofs and the heavy sound of a horse being urged through close-grown brush. Strang hugged the ground and swore behind clenched teeth. The man with the Winchester was a-horse and making a getaway out through the back of the timber stand.

Strang knew that his own pony and Nacio's were tethered too far away for him to mount up and ride after the sniper. He heard the crash of disturbed undergrowth and the pounding of the horse dwindle and die in the night.

He trudged back to the encampment in the rock cluster. The sodden ashes of the fire hissed sullenly and an icy bitterness took hold of Strang's whole being when he saw the manner in which Nacio was stretched in his blankets, wooden and lifeless. Squatting beside his partner's bedroll, Strang struck a match and studied the Mexican.

A Winchester bullet — it must have been the first one, fired from the timber the very moment Strang had called his warning and kicked over the coffee-pot — had drilled Nacio through the head as he slept. Strang saw that he had doused the meagre fire too late. The bushwhacker had already drawn a bead on Nacio and doubtless had Strang's bedded-down form lined up for his second shot. A hard chill took hold of Strang, seeping into the marrow of his bones.

So this was how their partnership ended and this how Star and Bar wanted to make its play, by sneaking up and shooting sleeping men!

He had little enough time for Star and Bar, but he never imagined the Tedrow outfit to be that low. Scaring a man off his land with threats and wild shooting was one thing, dead of the night murder was another.

'All right.' he told the corpse of his Mexican partner. 'If Tedrow and his crew want to fight this way, I'll match 'em, and I'll build a ranch on this land if I have to kill every Star and Bar rider to do it!'

Mechanically, he thumbed fresh shells into the empty chambers of his Colt, put on his boots and hat and walked slowly to his tethered pony. He had dumped his gunny-sack close to the animal earlier and he rummaged in it to find a battered old miner's shovel with only half a handle, a useful relic of the gold strike episode.

As dawn widened across the big sky, he buried Nacio Laca close to the rock cluster.

★ ★ ★

Strang took a lonely meal by the revived fire, drinking hot, strong coffee to dispel the lingering chill of horror which still gripped him. He made a check at the brush pen, assuring himself that the cattle were safely hemmed in, then he mounted his pony and rode up towards the timber stand from which the bushwhacker wrought his cowardly work the night before.

Up there, he dismounted and prowled

50

restlessly about the fringe of the trees until he located the position from which the dark-of-the-moon sniper had fired. At the margin of the timber, there was a big partially buried boulder, humping out of the ground like a buffalo's back and with saplings and brush closely grown around it. There were a couple of Winchester cartridge cases lying on the ground behind it.

Strang considered them with his mouth pulled into a critical line. Only two shells had been fired from here; the third must have been triggered from further into the timber stand. The bushwhacker probably changed his position when he realized that the man coming up the dark slope with a six-gun was drawing close upon him.

Rod noticed the imprints of a knee and a boot in the sandy earth just behind the rock — a right knee kneeling and a left foot planted on the ground as the sniper took aim. Strang put his own right knee into the impression in the sand and planted his left foot in the bootprint. Over the crest of the upward bulging boulder, he could see the rock cluster down the rise and the position was so elevated that he could look down into the centre of the cluster with ease. Picking off a man as he slept by the flames of a dying fire down there would not be difficult.

Then, Strang made a discovery. *He* could not have done it from the exact position occupied by the bushwhacker, because he was right handed and, to his right, the sheltering rock rose upwards, making it impossible for a right handed man to level a rifle at the rock cluster. But, at the left, it angled downwards and a man who habitually used his left hand could place his shots easily from this cover with the Winchester raised to his left shoulder.

'So I'm looking for a left handed man!' mused Strang as he went back to his tethered pony.

He rode through the trees in the hope that he might pick up the trail of the man who had made a horseback plunge out of them the night before, but the trees were so closely grown and the ground so tangled with brush that picking up the trail was a hopeless proposition. Strang continued riding and musing.

The timber thinned and he was soon riding down the far slope of the rise, through pinons and white oaks. The sun was climbing high into the azure sky and there was a dry but not wholly unpleasant wind coming off the nearby desert flats.

Strang stiffened in his saddle as the wind bore two brief sounds to him. One was the panicky snort of a horse and the other an ill-defined squeak, like a sudden voicing of alarm.

He wheeled his pony. The sounds had come from over on his right where the timber was thicker and the land obviously more fertile. Strang spurred his pony deep into the trees. He heard the screech of the horse again. He turned his mount's nose in the direction of the sound and covered ground fast.

4

Strang paced the pony through the crowding trees at a dead-run and burst out into a downward slanting, tract of land which dropped steeply to a swiftly flowing stream. Down by the water, a girl in a white shirtwaist and riding skirt was struggling to stay in the saddle of a panicky bay gelding.

The animal was pitching its forelegs high, whinnying loudly and the girl, sunlight burnishing the braided golden hair of her uncovered head, was fighting with the rein and trying to soothe the gelding verbally. She partially succeeded, managing to cajole the animal to plant its forelegs down and hold a jittery stance, but her mount suddenly gave an unexpected upward thrust which all but jerked her out of the saddle. Then, snorting furiously, he took off along the dark, loamy fringe of the stream at a thundering gallop, the girl holding her place in the leather magnificently.

Rod Strang had halted his pony close to the margin of trees. He watched the golden headed rider battle with the frightened gelding, admiring her staying power then, with a curious slow-motion movement, the gelding was crumpling down forefeet first to the boggy soil at the edge of the noisy stream. Two things registered on Strang's brain, the distinct crack of breaking bone and the sight of the girl being pitched over the animal's head, her shrill scream dying as she was swallowed dramatically by the foaming fury of the water.

Strang put his pony into a streaking run, then hauled leather to drag it to a slithering, splay-footed halt, mauling the loam at the water's edge into furrows. He came down from the saddle, pitching off his hat and pausing to make a fumbling, impatient business of pulling off his scuffed boots.

Rod felt a shock as violent as a

physical blow to the stomach when he realized that the girl had completely disappeared. He took in the brawling sweep of the turbulent stream, saw that it twisted away several yards from where he stood, swinging behind a stand of timber. At the point where the water met the timber, it roiled over a jumble of rocks with a roar which spoke of hidden falls.

Abruptly, Strang saw a brief flurry of the girl's grey riding skirt amid the swiftly running, foam-creamed water close to the rocks. He caught sight of the golden hair, had a brief glimpse of her face, then she was gone under the surface once more. The brief glimpse was sufficient to indicate to Strang that she was unconscious and that the grasping current was dragging her along as easily as it would a straw. She would either be dashed against the piled-up rocks or hauled over them to be swept over the falls which roared beyond.

Strang went into the water in a

speedy if clumsy dive. The water was unexpectedly deep for an Arizona stream even this early in summer, and Strang allowed himself to be tugged into mid-stream by the current, kicking out in a strong crawl, moving with the tugging water towards the string of rocks.

The bellowing of the falls grew in his ears and the volume of the sound indicated that the falls were high. Near-panic gripped him at the thought that the young woman might already have been pitched over the drop. He began to tread water against the strong haul of the stream, shook his head like a wet terrier and sought the girl. He saw floating skeins of yellow hair where the water swirled around the rocks.

The girl had been jounced out of the main stream and had come to rest like a fragment of driftwood in the eddies foaming amid the scatter of rocks. Even as Strang marked her position, he could see that she was slowly being dragged back into the main current and she was only a matter of yards away from a gap in the rocks — a gap which served as a wide doorway to the echoing falls beyond the barrier of sun-split stones.

With blood pounding at his temples, Strang struck out downstream. The crashing of the nearby falls made a roaring theme-song for his urgent, furious effort to fling his body downstream and reach the girl before she was swept through the gap in the rocks and over the falls.

Already, she was drifting into the gap. The white shirtwaist, the grey riding skirt and the tangled mass of golden hair were visible as isolated splashes against the roiling foam in the turbulent region of the falls. Strang reached the rocks, snorting and straining for breath, putting all his strength into a quick lunge forward to grasp the girl under the armpits.

He began a backward-swimming battle with the tug of the stream, hauling the girl through the churning water, striving to keep her nose and mouth clear of the surface. The water seemed possessed of a million grasping hands which sought to thrust the pair over the roaring drop, but Strang kicked back at them furiously. Slowly, he pulled himself and the girl free of the main stream and made a weary progression towards the shore.

With his strength all but sapped, Strang hauled the girl clear of the stream and dumped her on the loamy bank, face downwards. He flopped down beside her, coughing up water and fighting for breath. He put the coughing fit over him and gulped air into his lungs. When he could breathe regularly and think clearly, he dragged himself up to a kneeling position to look at the girl.

She was breathing and water was bubbling from her mouth and nose. As Strang watched her, she gave a shudder and a spluttering cough and suddenly came alive, rolling over to look up at Strang in a dazed fashion. She was sobbing deeply, trying to catch her breath.

'You're all right,' said Rod Strang huskily. 'Lie there awhile until you can breathe easily.'

The girl's golden hair was plastered about a curiously elfin face with high cheekbones and wide set eyes. The eyes were blue and, even in the girl's present predicament, they held an expression all their own. There was determination and resolution in them, but also a hint of mischief. In the slightly upturned nose, there was a touch of tomboy. She was not at her most presentable, lying beside the stream in sodden clothing and with her hair straggling in wet rat-tails, but a man would have to be made of stone not to be attracted to this girl.

There was a bruise over her right eye, making a darkening patch of discolourations. She sat up slowly, obviously trying to gather her wits.

'You pulled me out of there?' she asked, nodding towards the stream.

'Yes,' said Strang. 'Your gelding pitched you in. You seem to have hit your head on a rock when you went under. You were unconscious, but I'd say you'll be sound enough in a minute or so.'

She passed a hand over her brow.

'Mv head aches — I seem to remember being thrown — it's all like a dream. Thanks again for pulling me out.'

'It was nothin', ma'am,' Strang replied. 'Just a fortunate thing I came along when I did. Better sit there awhile and catch your breath. I have a little thing to take care of.' He stood up and the girl said sharply: 'Where are you going?'

Strang answered slowly: 'I don't want you to make any fuss about this, ma'am, but I'm going to find my pony to collect my rifle from the saddle-scabbard; my Colt won't work until I dry out the shells. I'll have to go back upstream to yore cayuse and shoot him. He broke a leg.'

'I won't make any fuss,' answered the girl levelly. 'I know as much about horses as you and I know how they have to be treated. It's a pity. I hoped I would cure that animal of its nervousness and make a smart mount of it. Hurry back upstream and put the poor thing out of its misery!'

Rod Strang trudged wetly along the margin of the stream, reflecting on the girl's solid common sense. He found his pony cropping grass and, downstream, the girl heard the single sharp crack of his carbine.

She was still sitting beside the stream when Strang, paced back along the water's edge. She was smoothing her bedraggled hair with slender fingers. The sun was already drying out her clothes in patches. Strang led his pony towards her.

Strang stood over her and said: 'You should get back wherever you belong tolerably quick, miss. You could catch a chill or something. Take my pony and ride him home. I have another one a little ways back. It belonged to my partner but he won't require it any more.'

The girl looked up at him sharply.

'Why won't your partner require the pony?' she asked.

'He's dead,' stated Rod drily. 'Somebody shot him when we were bedded down last night.' By way of changing the subject, he asked: 'How far do you have to ride, ma'am?'

The girl stood up slowly and fixed Strang with a stare that was all defiance. She said in a flat voice: 'To Star and Bar headquarters. My name's Jane Tedrow.'

Rod felt an involuntary gasp sigh out of him. Dimly, from the days of his boyhood, came the memory that Cal Tedrow had a small daughter — a girl who would be around Rod's own age. So this was she, a child no longer.

Strang said, mechanically: 'So you're the daughter of the owner of Star and Bar!'

'I *am* the owner of Star and Bar,' she responded crisply. 'My father died four years ago — just got sick and died in bed — perhaps you didn't know that, Mr Strang!'

'I didn't,' he said. It came as a blow almost as forceful as the death of Ignacio Laca. For years, he had built up plans to fight Star and Bar. For years, Star and Bar had been represented by the image of bushy bearded Cal Tedrow. Now, Tedrow was dead and Star and Bar was owned by a pretty and obviously spirited slip of a girl. He could have fought Colonel Cal Tedrow, but how could he fight a mere girl?

While he was looking blankly into Jane Tedrow's face, she said, with a sharp edge to her voice: 'You're Strang, the man who had the gall to ride on to Star and Bar land and put beef on it. You'd better move that beef pretty quick, Mr Strang. Move it and clear out of this country!'

Strang shook his head.

'The beef stays there and I stay too. Especially now that I'm looking for a man,' he told her flatly.

'The man who killed your partner?'

'The same, and I happen to think he is a Star and Bar rider.'

Hot anger flared in Jane Tedrow's eyes.

'You're wrong. My riders don't go in for bushwhacking sleeping men. I can answer for every one of them. Whoever shot your friend was not working for me.'

'Star and Bar riders go in for running defenceless men off land legally filed over to them, don't they?' responded Rod harshly. 'They did that to my father twelve years ago. They ran him off the land where I'm squatting now. That land is not Star and Bar's. I checked at the government land offices at Phoenix and it's still registered under my father's name. That's why I'm stayin' there. Your bunch is welcome to try runnin' me off or backshootin' me, but you can take warnin' that I aim to stay.'

They stood scowling at each other for a moment and Strang added lamely: ''Course, I have nothin' personal against you, Miss Tedrow, I want you to understand that.'

The girl's expression softened slightly, but there was still defiance in her eyes.

'And I want you to understand that my men are not wanton killers. There are things we should talk over in more comfortable surroundings than this. Maybe we'll have a chance when you come to Star and Bar to pick up your pony.'

'Is that an invitation?' asked Strang.

'It is, but on condition that you behave yourself and don't push any of my hands in the dirt as you did in town yesterday,' Jane Tedrow stated.

'I'm only likely to become objectionable if I meet the man who murdered Nacio Laca on your spread,' Strang answered.

The girl noted the way he stood with his right hand hanging slack over the handle of his holstered six-gun. She shook her head and there was something close to grief in her face.

'How can this territory ever become peaceable if men are to continue taking the law into their own hands?' she demanded. 'There's a marshal in San Junipero and it's his business to deal with lawbreakers. Why don't you go and see him?'

Strang gazed at her coldly. 'You own the biggest cattle-outfit in this vicinity and I'm a saddle-tramp who, according to your version, is trespassing on your grass. When I was a kid, they used to say that Cal Tedrow owned San Junipero and everything in it. You probably inherited it — including the marshal. What sort of a deal is your precious law-man going to give me?'

'You're a suspicious, stubborn man. You don't deserve help from anyone!' Jane Tedrow answered cuttingly. 'Give me that pony. I'm going home before I catch a chill!'

Rod Strang watched the slender form of the daughter of Cal Tedrow ride away from him and disappear into the crowding timber. Long after she had gone, he was still standing in the sunlight, deep in thought.

5

It was almost noon when Rod Strang rode into San Junipero on Nacio Laca's cow-pony. He went at an easy pace along the rutted and fouled street. paying little attention to the few miners, Mexicans and Indians who loafed in the scant shade of the warped awnings roofing the boardwalks.

He headed the pony in the direction of a building he remembered seeing from the corner of his eye when he and Ignacio arrived in town with their beef-on-the-hoof; a building of solid, sun bleached adobe, standing apart from the stores, saloons and houses. In flaking red paint, the words 'United States Marshal' were lettered across the adobe over the door lintel. Under them, in newer paint, was the name: 'Daniel Warren'.

Strang rode towards the law office

reflecting on the point that maybe there was a semblance of order coming to this region after all. So far as he remembered, there wasn't an officer of the law around San Junipero when he'd been here as a youngster — the town and its neighbouring lands nudged the desert in a scantily mapped and almost forgotten section of Arizona Territory. He entered town burning with curiosity. The girl had mentioned a marshal. Maybe he was her marshal, in the grasp of the Star and Bar outfit in the way most things in San Junipero had been in the grasp of her father before her. But he represented the law and Rod Strang determined to see what the law looked like — and discover with whom its sympathies lay.

There was a tall, youngish man leaning idly against one of the uprights of the marshal's office gallery as Strang reined up. He watched Strang's approach with interest and now he stood upright, walking a few paces to the gallery steps and halting at the top of them.

His eyes were fixed on the newcomer as Strang looped his pony's rein around the hitchrack and his mouth was curled back in a curious mixture of animosity and pleasure. Strang was busy at the hitchrack with his back to the man on the gallery when the man called: 'Hey, you! Come here!'

There was an insulting inflection in the voice.

Rod whirled about and took in the details of the man on the gallery of the office for the first time.

He was tall and well built and might have been anything from twenty six to thirty. The bright sunlight put a golden patina on his worn clothing, inelegant but serviceable range clothing, and it glittered on the star on his buckskin vest. It was the star of a US Marshal, not a deputy, and a Navy Colt was holstered low on the man's left thigh.

A spider-legged chill crawled up Rod Strang's spine when he saw that the marshal had lost his right arm. The empty sleeve was pinned up to his faded shirt and the memory of the evidence which showed that Nacio Laca had been murdered by a left handed man flooded back to Strang.

'I said come here!' rasped the law officer. 'I want to talk to you.'

Strang strode languidly towards the gallery steps.

'And I want to talk to you,' he responded. 'Why else would I pull up here?'

'I'll talk first,' the marshal said grimly. 'You're the *hombre* who pulled a gun out on the street yesterday — I hear you pulled it tolerably fast. Then you pushed Orde Clemmins on his tail-end in the dirt.'

Strang had mounted three of the four steps giving on to the gallery of the lawman's office and the pair now stood face to face. Rod saw that the marshal's face, under the shade of his off-white sombrero, was darkly handsome and as tough and determined as any he'd ever seen.

'That's right,' he told the lawman

quietly. 'I did that. I think I'd do it again if anyone interfered with my business.'

The one-armed marshal remained quite rigid, but his hand was held languidly over the butt of his Navy Colt. A tough grin was spreading over his face, but his eyes were cold.

'I'll tell you something, friend,' he began with a purr in his voice. 'I don't like gunslicks, there are too many of your kind around here lately, and I don't like fellows who create disturbances in my town. I was out of town yesterday when you happened along. But now I'm in town.' He paused and Strang saw the lids come down to hood his eyes and when he spoke next, the marshal hissed the words through his teeth: 'This time, *I'm* interferin' with yore business!'

Strang felt a cold twist at his innards. This cripple with a law-star was deliberately prodding him into a gunfight.

He stared hard into the dark,

belligerent face of the peace officer. A memory from the past rose before him, the memory of his father with his crippled hand and the way the Star and Bar rannihans picked on him. Strang hated them for riding roughshod over a man who didn't have a fighting chance and he knew he'd hate himself if he drew his gun on this one-armed marshal.

'Kind of pushin' it, ain't you, Marshal?' he said quietly. 'I said I came here to talk with you. I wanted to talk about my partner who was murdered last night on what I believe is your jurisdiction.' He paused then, remembering the evidence pointing to a left handed killer, and added grimly: 'But I'm not sure you don't know all about it already.'

'I don't know what you're talkin' about,' snarled the lawman, 'but if yore partner was the same gunslingin' kind as you, there'll be no tears for him in this country.' His single hand was still hovering over the butt of his Navy Colt and his eyes were smouldering. Strang knew from those eyes that this marshal was as dangerous a man as he ever saw; he knew he was going to continue bulldogging him into a pistol fight, and he knew he could not draw on a man who wore one sleeve pinned to his shirt.

'I aim to clear out every one of you gunhands who've shown up in this country in recent weeks, Mister,' said the marshal in a low and almost confidential tone. 'And there's one thing I want to see right now, that quick draw of yore's that set this town talkin' yesterday. I'm callin' you, Mister!'

A ripple of excitement crisped through the little knot of idlers that had gathered around the steps of the marshal's office and several hastened away from the immediate vicinity of the men on the gallery steps.

'I'm not pullin' my gun on you, Marshal,' said Strang icily. 'No matter how hard you push me.'

'Not even if I push you *this* hard?' asked the peace officer, and he brought his hand up to give Rod a forceful, stinging slap across the mouth. Strang rocked back and almost lost his footing on the steps. Through sudden tears, he saw the marshal looming before him. He heard the man's snarling words:

'I'll teach you and yore kind to come infestin' this part of the territory with yore presence an' yore smart-alecky ideas!'

He slammed a bunched fist at Strang's jaw in a sledge-hammer blow which sent him flying backwards clear off the gallery steps. The coarse, sun-warmed and horse-fouled dirt of the street seemed to leap up and crash into Strang's back. He lay at the bottom of the steps, his head exploding into vivid stars and blinding lights and the salty issue from a cut lip almost choking him.

Painfully, he dragged himself up and became dimly aware that men were crowding around, but keeping at a respectful distance, making a crude arena for the marshal and him. And the peace officer was there, looming in front of him again.

Through a tear-dimmed, swimming red haze, he saw the lawman's face and the marshal panted: 'We haven't finished yet, not by a long way. You're goin' to be sorry you ever heard of San Junipero!'

There was a growl of anticipation from the crowd and it came to Strang's befuddled brain that the townsfolk had seen something like this before. One-armed or not, this law-dog was a fighter and he delighted in a scrap. He was going to give the town a show and the townsfolk were looking forward to it.

Strang tried to steady his wobbling legs, but the lawman was suddenly on him like a tornado. He hit Strang across the jaw again, followed the blow with a cuff across the ear, waited until Rod quit teetering backwards, then sailed into him with a piledriver to the midriff which gusted every atom of wind out of him.

Rod jack-knifed, scooted back on his

heels and hit the dirt again, sending a section of the yelling crowd hustling backwards as he slithered against their boots.

He rolled over and lay face down in the dirt for a long, painful moment, then he hauled himself slowly upwards into a crouch. He tried to think straight and the persistent notion that the man who was beating the daylights out of him — a man whom he could not fight because of his disability — was the one who had fired on Nacio Laca from the cover of the trees kept suggesting itself at the back of his mind. The feverish desire for vengeance flared high in Strang and he wobbled upwards on legs of jelly.

The one-armed marshal was standing a yard away, braced with legs a-spraddle and fist bunched for the next onslaught. Strang saw him through a swimming murk and he tottered forward towards the peace officer, spurred by a half-crazed desire for revenge; revenge for the humiliation of this punishment, handed out before the whole town, but mostly revenge for the killing of Nacio. As Strang moved, he deliberately planted his right hand behind his back. He mustered all his strength and expended it in a forward leap which brought him upon the marshal with his left arm flailing.

He chopped a lucky blow across the lawman's jaw. Through the sound of blood roaring at his temples, he heard his adversary snort with pain. Strang could scarcely see the other man, but he went stubbornly in towards the dim outline of a faded shirt and off-white sombrero, left arm jabbing and swiping.

Somewhere, miles away it seemed, he could hear the whooping and yelling of an excited crowd; but there was a dream-like quality to the distant din as there was a dream-like quality to all things around him. His mouth was full of blood and there was a roaring in his ears. The shirt and sombrero of his opponent were only half-perceived things, but Strang kept flailing out at them.

The marshal came fighting back. He sledged punches at Strang, well-placed, heavy punches, every one calculated to wear the near exhausted man down. The watching mob yelled with unbridled excitement as the two men traded blows.

Strang fought down the desire to stick up both fists and fight in the manner to which he was accustomed, using his right arm as a guard and leading with his left, but there was something in him which said he must fight a disabled man on his own terms. He continued lashing out, one-handed, occasionally contacting with the law officer, but mostly missing wildly.

He spluttered and snarled and felt himself sinking into a swimming daze — and still the merciless punches of his one-armed adversary swung in at him from beyond the waves of dizziness. He tottered against the lawman, clutching at his shoulder for support, and still keeping his right arm behind his back.

The marshal allowed him to rest

there for a moment, then he shoved the weight of the half-conscious Strang away from him, steadied him on his sagging legs and planted the palm of his hand full in Strang's face in precisely the way Strang had planted his in Orde Clemmins's face the day before. For a little while, they held a comical pose, the unsteady Strang being supported with his face against the other's hand like a comic on the vaudeville stage. Then, the peace officer shoved him backwards with all his force.

The mob of townsfolk that had increased rapidly since the mêlée began, roared with harsh-voiced delight as Rod Strang flopped heavily into the dirt with less dignity than a rag doll.

This time, he lay motionless on his back.

He was almost out, but not quite. He had the impression that the marshal was standing over him and he heard harsh words rasped at him:

'You better take yoreself away from here, *muy pronto*, gunslick. Yoreself an' that beef you had the gall to put on Star and Bar grass. Next time I have occasion to clash with you. I'll kill you!'

Even in his semi-delirium, Strang reflected that the reference to Star and Bar gave him some indication as to whom the lawman favoured — but did he favour Jane Tedrow's outfit enough to go out and kill trespassers on Star and Bar land, shooting from ambush?

The marshal spoke again, making another reference to gunhands in the vicinity: 'You can tell any of those reputation gunslicks that seem to be slippin' into this country that the marshal of San Junipero is hell on big-name trigger trippers, as well as on cheap skates like you. Show 'em yore bruises if they doubt it!'

Rod managed to pull himself upwards and remained sprawled in the dirt with the upper part of his body canted up and supported on his elbows. He was trying to force his hazy brain to make sense of what the peace officer had said. It was not the first time he had referred to gunmen coming into this locality.

With impaired vision, Strang saw that the crowd was thinning away and that the one-armed law officer was standing triumphantly over him. There was a trickle of blood from his nose, but he still wore his hat and his shirt seemed scarcely to have been ruffled since the moment Strang first saw him on the gallery of his office. The lawman turned his back scornfully and strode away towards the sun-splashed adobe structure of his office.

A woman's voice, charged with emotion, suddenly shrilled from across the street.

'Dan Warren, you should be ashamed of yourself!'

The marshal halted and turned about. Strang twisted his head towards the direction from which the voice came. He could dimly see the form of a young woman leaning over the gallery rail of a store building almost opposite the marshal's office.

'You shouldn't have treated him that

way,' she called to the peace officer. 'I saw it all and I'm disgusted with you, Dan Warren. He didn't want to fight you and when he had to fight, he was man enough to meet you on your own terms!'

The marshal gave a harsh laugh.

'Man! Don't get carried away with emotion, Ruthie. He's yellow as a snake's belly — his kind are all yellow under the big gunhand showmanship!'

'Not this one,' answered the girl. 'He has chivalry — and you must be blind if you can't see it!'

The marshal gave a loud hoot of derision.

'Chivalry! I declare you've been readin' fairy stories, Ruthie! This *hombre* is no handsome prince. Go back to your cookin', girl, that's a business you understand right well — and leave the business of tamin' this town to me!'

He turned and resumed the journey back to his office and Strang, still sprawled in the middle of the street, became aware of the approaching rustle of skirts. The girl who had shouted to the marshal approached him and squatted down beside him. He looked up into a serious face, heart-shaped with jet black hair brushed neatly back from it, looking into his.

'Can you stand up and walk?' asked the girl.

'Maybe, if I try very hard,' commented Rod wryly.

'Then come across to my eating house. I'll clean you up. You're cut and bruised terribly — your face looks like a butcher's shop!'

The girl hoisted him to his feet with the businesslike air of a mother managing a child. Strang grinned at her weakly and staggered alongside her in the direction of the store from which she had hailed the marshal.

6

A sign over the door read: 'THE SUNSET EATING HOUSE' in black capitals and the girl led the way up the scuffed wooden steps, across the gallery and into the building. Strang went in her wake on rubbery legs.

Business appeared slack, for all it was noon. The neat tables, each with a clean cloth draped over it, which stood down the centre of the eating house, were all unoccupied. There was a counter running the length of one wall and behind it was a mirror. Strang had a mild shock when he saw his reflection. His face was battered and bruised and his hair straggled in sweat-plastered tails over his eyes. His crumpled range-garb, which bore evidence of the ducking he had taken earlier that day to pull Jane Tedrow out of the stream, was caked with the dirt of the street. It occured to him that he had lost his hat but, for the first time, he noticed that the girl had retrieved it from the street. She waved it in the direction of a chair, then shied it with satisfactory results at a tall hatstand in one corner.

'Sit down,' she invited. 'I don't think we'll have many customers. I usually do a coffee and doughnut trade at this time of day. Evening is the time the people around here like to eat in a big way. I get the miners coming in in droves after they quit.'

Strang liked the way she spoke. There was an easy lilt to her voice and a slight drawl, but her words were formed with a precision which suggested a good background and education. She seemed out of place running an eating house for miners, but it was plain to see that something of her own neat orderliness was reflected in the premises.

He watched her go behind the counter and out through a small door into what he guessed was the kitchen. His head was beginning to clear, but he still felt as though a snorty Texas herd had trampled him down. Nevertheless, his brain was beginning to work well enough to appreciate the girl the marshal had called Ruthie.

He liked everything about her. She was slender and taller than the average woman but well enough built to carry the extra inches with dignity. Her hair was nightblack and had a rich thickness. It was brushed back and braided into a bun at the nape of her neck. The girl's complexion had a fresh glow and her skin was not yet dried out by the Southwestern air; her face was moulded in cleanly formed planes and her dark eyes held common-sense and sympathy.

She came back from behind the counter carrying a bowl of water and a cardboard box was gripped under one arm. She walked towards Rod in a brisk, businesslike way, looking cool and efficient in her light blue dress with a spotless apron tied around the waist. Rod looked away quickly, feeling a touch of guilt that he should stare at her so intently. She was worth staring at, as any man would have to admit.

He wondered why a woman should go to such trouble for a man who was a total stranger and who looked a gun-hung tramp, as he now knew he looked, having studied himself in the mirror behind the counter. She stood over him and began to swab at a gash at the corner of his mouth with a cloth soaked in warm water from the bowl. There was a tantalizing perfume from her hair.

'You're very kind,' said Strang in warm appreciation as she clapped a strip of court plaster over the wound. 'Especially considerin' I'm a stranger an' not of good character, accordin' to your marshal.'

'Humph!' the girl grunted, shrugging her shoulders. 'I've patched up all kinds after brawls. It's a knack I have and I don't like seeing people get hurt. You grown men behave so often like little boys, it's a pity I can't spank you as well as clean you up!' She dropped her voice to a more serious tone. 'In your case, though, I liked the way you fought Dan Warren on his own terms. You were a fool to try it, but that's the kind of fool I like. You didn't want to fight him, did you?'

'No. I once saw a bunch of fellows pick on a man with only one good hand and I wouldn't want to be tarred with the same brush as that particular bunch.'

The girl washed caked blood from his face.

'That's what I call chivalry, no matter how Dan Warren laughs. I can't think you're the kind of man he says you are, a gunfighter.'

'I'm not.' he told her. 'I can use a gun, but I'm not the reputation gunslinger Warren seems to think I am. The only time I made a livin' with my gun was when I was doin' the kind of job he's doin'. Any men I shot then needed shootin'!'

'I thought you were pretty square, Mr — '

'Strang. Rod Strang.'

She placed another strip of plaster across a cut in his brow, then straightened up.

'I'm Ruth Calton. My father owns this place, but I run it.' She paused to pack plaster and cotton wool back into the box, then said: 'By the way, don't get Dan Warren wrong. He's all right, but he's mean on gunmen — he has a bee in his bonnet about them, 'specially in the last few weeks. Several gunslingers have been showing up in the country. Dan thinks there's something afoot. Don't let his one arm fool you; he can take care of himself.'

'You're tellin' me!' commented Rod, rubbing his sore jaw. 'He piled himself at me like a crazy bronc.'

'That's the way he does things,' Ruth said. 'He just wades in and takes his chance. Sometimes, I think it's because he figures he should be dead anyway.'

Rod lifted his eyebrows in interrogation.

'He was a cavalry sergeant a few

years back. He was with a company that was jumped by Geronimo's Apaches over in the Dragoons,' she went on. 'The officer was killed and so were many of the men. The Indians were using Winchesters which had been supplied to them by whites. Dan had his right arm riddled by bullets, but he somehow managed to get the remnants of the company out of the ambush and take his wounded down to Fort Huachuca. The surgeon at the fort had to take off his arm to save his life.'

Strang grunted and thought privately: *Maybe it was a man who learned about ambushes from Apaches who was holed up over our camp last night!* He had come into town to find out where the marshal's loyalties lay, if they lay anywhere outside his strict duty to the people who had elected him. Now, he figured he knew. There was little use in complying with Jane Tedrow's suggestion that the marshal should be told of Nacio's death.

He had intended talking to the

marshal about it, but Warren sprang at him like a wild animal before the business was even started. Warren had told him to move his beef off Star and Bar land, so Warren could be marked as a Star and Bar man. And Warren, he figured, was the left handed man who had holed up in the timberline and fired on their camp last night.

But there was one awkward aspect which stubbornly refused to slot into Strang's theory; a man with Dan Warren's fighting cavalry courage, one who had the guts to call a gun-hung stranger of unknown potential to draw his pistol, was not the kind to use night ambush tactics!

It was a fact that had to be faced. Rod Strang faced it and pondered over it. Ruth Calton broke his thoughts, asking: 'Would you like some coffee?'

The question reminded Strang that he had not eaten since taking a scanty breakfast at the camp on Star and Bar's pastures that morning. He nodded and, when Ruth had prepared the coffee, he asked cautiously:

'Star and Bar must pack a lot of weight around here.'

She paused in pouring the rich stream of coffee into his cup, her dark brows curved into a frown and he noticed that she glanced at his thonged-down holster before she asked: 'What makes you enquire?'

He shrugged and said lightly: 'Nothin'. It just occurred to me that it seems a tolerably big spread, big an' important.'

She resumed pouring the coffee.

'It was important once, when the old colonel was alive. That was before Dad and I came out here. Now, I understand, it's crewed by old retainers, most of them loyal but ageing men who fought with Colonel Tedrow in the war. The colonel's daughter owns the place, she's smart and capable, but a ranch needs a man to boss it.'

'Yeah,' agreed Strang. 'A pretty girl like Miss Tedrow deserves a husband to match.' He caught the unspoken question in Ruth's eyes and added: 'I made her acquaintance earlier today.'

'She'll have one, but he insists on serving out his term as marshal of this town first. He figures enforcing the law is a job for a single man,' she told him.

'Warren?' asked Strang and Ruth gave a positive nod.

Again, a question concerning the killing of his partner rose in Strang's mind: *would a man, even one with Warren's obvious courage, descend to bushwhacking men whom he considered to be trespassers on the land he one day hoped to marry into?*

Ruth disappeared behind the counter and out of the little door to return an instant later with a newly browned sweet potato pie. 'I think you'll enjoy this, if you can make your jaw work,' she suggested. Strang did enjoy it, in spite of having to eat it with care out of consideration for his aching jaw and cut mouth. He drank more coffee and rolled a smoke, then pushed the subject of Star and Bar as a power in this particular land.

'Star and Bar is not so good as it looks, huh?' he asked, making the question as casual as he could.

'I believe not, though I don't know too much about it,' Ruth replied. 'I did hear that some combine or other had made a bid for the outfit, but Miss Tedrow won't sell. Those fiery old Texans still keep up a big show, though. Sometimes I feel sorry for them. They bounce around town with plenty of gusto, but rumour has it their outfit is crumbling under their feet. I heard the colonel incurred a lot of debts in his lifetime and they aren't paid off yet.'

Curiously, a glow of sympathy had warmed in Rod Strang. He never thought he would ever feel sorry for Star and Bar, but then, he had not reckoned on returning to this country to find the whooping Texans of his youth toned down into ageing men or to find a Star and Bar rumoured to be crippled by debts. Circumstances, he reflected, could alter cases considerably.

'Maybe Jane Tedrow will be forced

into selling to that combine,' Ruth Calton observed sadly. 'I don't like cattle combines. I don't believe they're all honest. My father was ruined by his dealings with one up in Montana. That's why we came down here with what little money we had left and opened a safe business. But my father's a cowman, and his heart is broken. That's why you could walk into Joe Bannock's or one of the other saloons right now and find him propping up the bar.' There was a bitterness in the girl's words that made Strang think she was essentially lonely, and, as the daughter of the town drunk, humiliated. Maybe that was why she had spoken to him so freely.

'You'll find yore dad will pull out of it,' he offered by way of comfort. 'A cowman will hit the bottle once in a while, then come out of it right smart when he has to.'

Ruth smiled wanly. 'I'd like to think you're right, but I doubt it,' she answered. 'My father's been a bar-fly for too long. He's a standing joke around here.'

Rod stood up stiffly and moved for the hatstand. He was still sore and weary, but he felt the benefit of the girl's doctoring, the coffee and the pie. He thanked her awkwardly.

'Not at all,' she murmured. 'Won't you call again sometime?' She smiled and Rod Strang observed that he would walk barefoot across the Painted Desert on the hottest day of the century to see that smile again.

But it was an inward observation, made to himself.

7

After leaving the Sunset Eating House, Strang crossed the street slowly, making for the hitchrack outside the sheriff's office. He unhitched Nacio's pony, mounted and was wheeling the animal about in order to ride out of town the way he had entered, when he caught sight of the sign over Joe Bannock's saloon. Quite suddenly, he decided on a drink. Besides, a saloon was often a good place to poke around when you were looking for something — and Strang's visit to San Junipero had brought him more than a beating from the marshal. His talk with Ruth Calton had given him a yearning to know more about the present standing of Star and Bar, among other things.

As he rode down the street, he was aware of the eyes of passers-by fixed on him. With his bruised face and strips of court plaster, he was one of the current sights of San Junipero, he reflected. He was the fellow who had given the town some entertainment by allowing himself to be licked by the marshal.

He dismounted stiffly at Bannock's saloon, whirled his rein about the hitchrack and walked in with a stiff limp. The place was empty apart from a tall man in clean faded denims and shirt who was leaning across the bar in alcoholic conversation with the bartender. Rod strode up to the bar and leaned against it, watching the sole customer and the bartender from the corner of his eye.

Under the droop of his floppy sombrero, the customer's face was seamed, but still handsome. The straight nose and the clean line of his jaw were features he had seen reflected in another face during the past few minutes and it was plain to see that Ruth Calton had inherited her tall stature from her father. The bartender was fat with a face the colour of dough. He was mechanically wiping the bar with a cloth, pretending to be interested in the loud talk of Calton who was holding forth like a bad actor.

'Can't tell me anythin' about cows, Frank, I know 'em from A to Z!' he declared. 'Handled every kind. Had the best herds ever gathered and the best crew ever born and the best pasture that ever grew . . . '

The dough-faced barman was saying: 'Sure, George,' at intervals as though he had heard the tall man's talk many times before.

He turned his head towards Strang and Strang saw from his eyes that the bartender recognized him as the man who had taken a whipping from Warren and the same one who pushed Orde Clemmins and pulled a speedy gun outside this saloon the previous day. He put down his bar-rag and walked languidly towards Rod, leaving Calton in midsentence. Calton did not seem to mind, he twisted his body slightly in the direction of both men and bawled down the bar: 'It don't take much to ruin an honest cowman, no sir! One day you have it good and rich. Can afford to treat your wife good and send yore kid to a respectable school in the East — next day, you been rode over roughshod by men who grind you into the dirt for yore honesty. A couple of bad winters on the run is all it takes. You find yoreself with depleted herds an' bills to pay!'

'Sure, George,' grunted the barman, then, to Strang: 'What'll it be?' There was neither friendliness nor belligerence in his face.

'A whiskey,' ordered Strang. 'A big one — an' make it good stuff!'

The bartender produced a bottle with a reputable label and poured a glassful.

'Can't pay bills when you've had two dirt-poor roundups in succession!' declared Calton along the bar. 'Then, the big money men come in an' start squeezin' yore outfit. It don't take much to ruin you after they get up to their tricks, Frank.'

'Sure, George,' rumbled the barman, swiping at a fly with the bar-rag. To Strang, he said in a low, toneless murmur: 'He'll keep this up for another hour or so, then he'll go over to the other end of town an' drink the rotgut in the Mexican cantina there, until his daughter goes to haul him home. It's the same every day.'

Strang merely grunted and betrayed nothing of the sympathy he felt towards George Calton.

There was a step behind him and a voice Strang had heard before said: 'Good afternoon.'

Rod turned lazily to see the man who had addressed him on the street the previous day, the flashily dressed one who had told Strang he could use a man of his calibre. Strang eyed him coldly. He disliked the broad, bland face, the small eyes, the puffy mouth, the overdressed neatness of the man and the affectation of the beaver hat, a style which went out of fashion the previous decade.

'I thought it was you I saw come in here,' said the newcomer, establishing himself at the bar by Strang's side.

'So you followed me in,' commented Strang.

The other nodded and ordered a whiskey. Further along the bar, George Calton had subdued into a sullen silence.

'They tell me you had a run-in with the marshal,' commented the over-dressed one casually.

'I got laid out lower than the preacher's dog, but I don't see that it's any concern of yours,' answered Strang.

The other smiled enigmatically and toyed with his glass. When he spoke next, he dropped his voice to a more confidential tone.

'You put those cows of yours up on those high pastures of Star and Bar. Seems to me you're wasting your time. You can scarcely fight Star and Bar and hold that land for yourself. How would you like to associate yourself with a bigger concern, offering good opportunities for ambitious young men?' The man spoke through a continual bland smile. 'Seems to me we could come to a mutually satisfactory agreement, you and I.'

Strang was remembering the way this man came to him the previous day and said he could 'use him'. This sounded like another way of framing the same offer. Strang decided to push the man into his offer and save him sailing around the point with a deal of smooth talk.

'You're offering money? What sort of money?' he enquired abruptly.

'Fair remuneration for services rendered properly — ' began the bland one.

Strang cut him down in mid-sentence: 'If you mean you're offering gun-wages, Mister, say so!'

The over-dressed one cast a hasty glance over his shoulder towards Frank and the now silent Calton. 'Not so loud!' he cautioned. 'Now see here, young fellow. I'll be frank with you. You have a grudge against Star and Bar and now I heard Star and Bar bushwhacked your partner. I can understand that you want to get even with Star and Bar for that, but you can't fight the outfit alone. Now, I'm a partner in a Chicago cattle-company and I'm down here looking over the land as a preliminary to making a bid for certain holdings.' He paused to finish his drink and Rod said sharply:

'I don't believe you told me yore name.'

'Gilman, Amos Gilman.'

'Of the Claybury-Gilman Cattle Corporation,' grunted Rod. 'I've heard of yore company.'

'Indeed!' exclaimed Gilman. 'Then you'll know we're a particularly pushing concern.' He turned on the bland smile again. 'Well, you know what sometimes happens when a new concern — especially a big one — comes into a cattle region. Some of the older people, the more hotheaded of the men who pioneered the land, for instance, forget that cattle-raising is a business and they get to using unbusinesslike methods in what they are pleased to call 'protecting their land'. Therefore it often pays for a concern to have several capable men around who can meet that kind of opposition in the only way it can be met.'

'You put it very delicately, Mr Gilman,' Strang complimented. 'What you really mean is that long-established cowmen in a region you aim to take over get to shootin' an' you want a trigger-crew to shoot back. You aim to take over Star and Bar and you know I have a quarrel with the outfit so you want to hire my gun!'

Amos Gilman shuddered as though the suggestion was repugnant to him. 'You put it rather indelicately,' he complained.

'It's an indelicate business,' Rod said. 'You figure that because I have a grudge against Star and Bar — and presumably one against Marshal Warren, who looks like a Star and Bar man, I'm going to sling in my shootin' iron with yore forthcoming move. You figure it wrong. Any fight I aim to make, I'll make alone. As for the Claybury-Gilman outfit, it's a bunch of big crooks with no guts payin' gun-carryin' scum to do their killin' for them.'

Gilman's jaw sagged slightly.

'I know all about yore company,' continued Rod acidly. 'I know how it put the Walker brothers' Walking W outfit out of business in South Dakota. It bought up the smaller neighbouring ranches surroundin' the Walkers' outfit, packed them with gunnies, then opened a range-war on the Walking W lands. I was a town marshal on the fringe of that ruckus an' I saw somethin' of it — I saw Seth Walker's corpse after yore paid killers laid up for him on a back trail. You engineered that business neatly, Gilman — but you engineered the whole thing from start to finish so that other people did yore killin' for you!'

Gilman simply stood in silence, glaring at Rod. There was a hardness in his eyes which told Strang that his words had hit him forcibly. In the solid silence, Strang slapped down the price of another whiskey on the counter, took the drink from Frank and downed it at a single jerk. With slow deliberation, he put the glass back on the counter and turned to Gilman.

'No, Mr Gilman,' he said tartly. 'I don't think we can do any business together.' He turned and walked slowly out of the saloon to where his pony was hitched.

Amos Gilman stood for a long spell with his eyes fixed on the door through which Strang had departed then he, too, walked out into the sunshine of the street.

On his departure, George Calton, who had been glowering at Gilman's back from under the drooped brim of his hat and holding a rigid position against the bar, came to life. He unfolded his tall body from its stiff, leaning attitude like a man slightly drugged.

'Great thunder, Frank!' he exclaimed, suddenly shedding his drunken and doped air. 'Did you hear who that fellow is? He's been hangin' around town for some days past an' he's one of the partners in the Claybury-Gilman company!' Calton's lips closed tightly, as if to hold in an oath, then he murmured in a peculiarly flinty tone: 'It was the Claybury-Gilman outfit that as much as robbed me of my spread up in Montana!'

★   ★   ★

Dusk was sifting over the desert flats and far peaks of the Dragoon mountains when Rod Strang angled the cow-pony over the high pastures of the land claimed by Star and Bar, making for the ragged fuzz of the timberline. He rode with his mind preoccupied.

He recalled Marshal Dan Warren's incomprehensible talk about too many trigger-trippers showing up in this vicinity and he matched it with the newly learned fact that the Claybury-Gilman outfit, which had paid trigger-wages and promoted range wars in the past, was on the scene. Like a man setting up a line of figures for addition, he placed a third factor under those two: Ruth Calton's remark that a combine had made some sort of offer to Jane Tedrow for ownership of the Star and Bar.

The answer came out: *trouble!*

Big trouble was brewing here in the desert-edge ranges. Rod Strang had come looking for one kind of trouble, and to make trouble. But he had come to the edge of another kind of trouble; the vicious bullet-throwing of a cattle-man's war. It was plain as day to him, now that he knew the identity of the bland man in the beaver hat, that what was coming up around here was aggression by hired gunhands. It had happened before in remote regions. He remembered the hot fury of the Murphy-Chisum feud which had erupted in the blazing lands of New Mexico not long before, and the life-for-a-life bullet-trading which was even now going between the Grahams and the Tewksburys in that piece of Arizona which men called Pleasant Valley.

It was murderous and dirty. It was composed of the elements of ambush, backshooting and cowardly advantage; the things which had placed Nacio Laca in a lonely and unmarked grave. It was range war. And it was coming here!

Strang rode towards the camp which he and Nacio had made in the rocks with his battered face set in a savage scowl. Funny, the way things had changed in a few hours, he reflected. He'd been full of hate for Star and Bar ever since he was a kid. He'd had the hate confirmed and intensified by the killing of Nacio Laca, for he had been certain the bushwhacking was perpetrated on the orders of Star and Bar. But, now, he was almost sympathetic towards the outfit which rip-roaring old

Cal Tedrow had built up with his former Rebel riders. The spread was owned by a mere girl and manned by a crew of faithful old retainers. It would be in no shape to face the sort of deal the scheming and grasping Claybury-Gilman Corporation would hand out.

The streak of solid cowman in Strang was in sympathy with Star and Bar. Colonel Tedrow had run his father off the pastures at the fringe of Star and Bar grass, but the old days were gone and the colonel with them. It looked as though Jane Tedrow's outfit was going to do the running now — and the Claybury-Gilman company would almost make it look legal while hired gunslicks rampaged around the range.

Strang mulled over the portentous signs he had encountered in San Junipero as he rode. He recalled that Jane Tedrow had more or less invited him to Star and Bar headquarters to retrieve his cow-pony. He would go there and take a warning. His private feud would still stand, for he wanted the land he claimed was his father's and he wanted Nacio Laca's killer even more. But the squareshooting cattle-man in him would never allow him to see something in the nature of another Walking W range-war shape up over Jane Tedrow's head without giving her a warning.

At the foot of a rise, he came to a thin stream with a knot of cattle watering there. Star and Bar beef, he figured, and he watched carefully for Tedrow riders who might shoot first if they saw him on the range. There were no riders and, as Strang, neared the animals in the thickening gloom, he saw that the iron with which they were burned was not the Star and Bar, but his own Running S. He cursed quietly.

Someone — probably someone from Star and Bar — had loosed the cattle from the carefully prepared brush pen which he and Nacio had created. They had penned the beef into a wide section of land where ample water was provided by a tributary of the stream at which this clutter of his stock was now drinking. With the brush pen broken, the Running S cattle would wander free across the ranges and mingle with the Star and Bar stock. Strang rode through the dusk, thinking wryly that Star and Bar was not likely to hold a special round-up to allow him to cut out his beasts from those bearing Jane Tedrow's iron.

With his face in a sullen grimace, he prodded the pony up to the point where he and Nacio had made their fateful camp. Panniers and camp gear which Rod had left among the rocks close to the ashes of last night's fire had not been interfered with. Star and Bar men were not thieves, but they had scrambled his plans considerably by turning his beef at liberty to wander footloose and free.

He reached the remains of the pen, found the brush fencing flattened by the hoofs of cattle happy to go adrifting and inquisitive to see what lay on the other side of the hill. Up on a sandy patch on the side of a hillock where no liberated cows had wandered, he found the prints of three broncs. The riders who had turned his beef loose had obviously sat their saddles there awhile, watching the Running S beasts scatter out of the pen.

So, Star and Bar had scored one across him — scored a second blow, assuming that the killing of Nacio Laca was the work of Star and Bar. Rounding up the scattered Running S beef was an impossible task for a lone man, he reflected, but the sharpness was taken off the edge of this cut from Star and Bar by the knowledge of what was brewing in this country.

Strang yanked the nose of his pony around and hit a lick away from the desolate camp-site in the general direction of Star and Bar's headquarters.

He'd pay a call on Jane Tedrow right now, he told himself.

8

Star-sequined night cloaked the wide rangeland when Rod Strang reached Star and Bar headquarters after an hour and a half of steady paced riding. The place had the outer appearance of most Southwestern desert-fringe ranch houses, a low adobe house holding pride of place with timber barns, a bunkhouse and blacksmith shop placed around it. But, even in the darkness, Strang was aware of an unusual neatness and order to the place, imparted, he supposed, by the hand of a woman.

The yellow glow of oil lamps showed at the windows of the bunkhouse, but the only sign of life was the mournful cadence of a harmonica playing a song which had been warbled by dance hall girls all along the western frontier for at least the past five years:

When the curtains of night are
* pinned back by the stars,*
And the beautiful moon shines
* above.*

Strang swung out of his saddle,
secured his rein to a peeled pole cross
bar of a corral and walked towards the
ranch house with his spurs chiming a
ringing accompaniment to the harmonica in the bunkhouse. Brightly
flowered curtains, backed by the soft
light of the evening lamps, made the
windows of the ranch house warm and
inviting. As he mounted the wooden
steps of the gallery, Rod remembered
how he had thought of the Star and Bar
ranch as a hotbed of evil ever since his
boyhood days. Now, it seemed too
pleasant and decent a place to be
swamped by the kind of hell-bent
skullduggery he had seen loosed against
the Walker Brothers' Walking W outfit
in Dakota.

At the door, fitted with meshes to
keep the summer insects out of the

house, he tapped a sharp tattoo on the frame. Jane Tedrow opened the door, looking a different person from the bedraggled girl Strang had hauled out of the waters at the lip of the falls.

The lamplight at her back put a faint nimbus about her light hair and her trim figure was garbed in a smart gown, curving in at the waist and flowing out elegantly at the skirt. Strang saw something like surprise in her partially shadowed face. He removed his hat and bade her good evening.

'You've come for your pony,' said Jane. It was not a question. It was a flat statement and there was something almost sullen about it. Strang figured it was the matter of his cattle, deliberately set loose on the ranges by Star and Bar hands, which brought this quality to her voice. She probably thought he was here to make trouble about it. He nodded a terse affirmative and Jane said: 'Well, come in for a minute. Star and Bar is not entirely inhospitable. If you'd like some supper after your ride, you're welcome to some.'

Strang grunted a mildly surprised thanks. It was hard, he thought, to be really mad at someone who offered you a meal after a ride, even if they had set you the impossible chore of sorting out your own cattle from hundreds of head roaming free over vast tracts of range.

The interior of the house held the same signature of a woman's hand as the exterior much more boldly written. Hide covered easy chairs bore neat cushions and the lamp in the centre of a table set for supper shone brightly upon the ornaments placed on the mantel of the big fieldstone fireplace. Over the fireplace were two photographs in heavy gilt frames. One showed Colonel Tedrow, looking much younger and handsomer than Rod ever remembered him. His full beard was jet black and he was in Confederate uniform. There was sufficient defiant tilt to his broadbrimmed officer's hat to suggest a rough-riding Texas background. The second portrait showed a demurely smiling young woman of delicate beauty with fair hair fashioned in the ringlets of the sixties.

Strang looked at Jane Tedrow in the lamplight. She had a dark bruise on her brow as a relic of her mishap at the swift stream. He saw that the strong character of her face was the character of Colonel Tedrow translated into feminine terms, but her blonde beauty was inherited from her mother.

Jane waved towards the table and Strang saw for the first time that it was set for two people.

'I'm expecting a guest,' she explained, 'but he won't be here for a while. In any case, there's plenty for three.' She added, with a note of almost childish curiosity: 'What happened to your face?'

'I met a man who didn't like it.' answered Strang, suddenly acutely aware of his battered appearance and the strips of sticking plaster. 'He decided to alter it for me.'

Jane sniffed and Strang was hard put to it to decide whether she was disgusted or amused. But there was no amusement in her voice when she spoke next, changing the subject abruptly: 'I suppose you want to lodge a complaint about my boys turning your cattle loose while you're here. Well, my boys *did* turn them loose and they did so on my orders. And, if you were clever and fortunate enough to round them all up and pen them in again, I'd have them all turned free at the first opportunity. You're squatting on my land, Mr Strang, and I don't like it!' There was tough defiance in her face and Rod was, paradoxically, glad to see she meant what she said. She was a fighter. That was good, she was going to need fighting spirit if the signs he had lately seen in this vicinity gave a true indication of what he thought was coming up.

'I don't want to make an issue about my cattle, Miss Tedrow,' he said, settling into a chair at the table. 'I came to collect my pony, and to give you a warning.'

'A warning?' she echoed blankly.

'About something I believe is brewing on these ranges. It's something I've seen before and I don't think you or anyone else in this country has fully cottoned on to it. I wouldn't want it to be loosed at you full tilt without any warning.' He spoke quietly and there was an underlying sincerity to his voice which claimed her attention. She settled in a chair across the table and asked:

'What do you mean?'

'Amos Gilman has been here to make you an offer for this spread, hasn't he?'

The girl began to put up a defensive wall.

'I don't see that it's any concern of yours — ' she began with high indignation.

'I know he was here,' cut in Strang. 'I've heard it rumoured that Star and Bar is in low water, that you have debts around yore neck and you're struggling to keep yore outfit alive. I don't much care if the rumours are true, but I guess they are because a big outfit in deep trouble is the type of outfit for which the Claybury-Gilman concern is likely to make a bid.'

'What if Mr Gilman has been here?' Jane queried with the note of indignation still in her voice. 'I won't sell and I told him that plain enough. The Star and Bar ranch will find its own way out of its difficulties. I won't sell out what my father struggled to build. Why, my father and his men fought Apaches — '

'Yeah, yeah, I've heard that one before,' put in Strang with a touch of cynicism. 'Has the Claybury-Gilman Corporation bought up any neighbouring ranches?'

'Yes, the Three Sixes, which joins our land over at Salt Ridge; the Box Triangle, over to the east and the Lazy K, in the west, all small ranches.'

'In other words, there is now Claybury-Gilman land on three sides of yours. If Claybury and Gilman bought up yore grass, they'd have a huge spread made up of all the good grass on this edge of the desert?'

Jane nodded and Rod fell silent for a moment. He was thinking of the way the Claybury-Gilman concern bought up small spreads around the Walking W in Dakota and packed them with gunslinging ruffians before making trigger talk against the unswerving Walker brothers who refused to sell out to the big company.

'Any common water shared by you and these other outfits?' he asked.

'Plenty. There are lots of small springs starting up in Salt Ridge and flowing down to water our land, but the most important is the creek that crosses our northern pastures. That starts up in Three Sixes land also. We have had water agreements with the other outfits for years.'

'The Claybury-Gilman outfit may not always see fit to honour old agreements,' commented Rod. Behind the remark, he was remembering that the range war in Dakota was stirred into flaring life by a dispute over water rights, engineered by the Claybury-Gilman faction.

'I still don't see what concern of yours my dealings with the Claybury-Gilman company can be,' Jane said acidly.

'I think the Claybury-Gilman outfit is going to prod trouble in yore direction,' Strang answered levelly. 'It's done so in the past an' I think it's goin' to do so again. I figure that, pretty soon, you'll have a parcel of hired gunsharps prancin' around here while Claybury and Gilman pull the strings in Chicago. I just wanted to warn you — whatever else is between us — I was on the edge of a Claybury-Gilman range-war once, an' it was unpleasant. A lot of people, includin' ranch women and children, suffered. I wouldn't want it to happen here.'

'For a man who thinks my outfit killed your partner — which it didn't — I must say you're very considerate, Mr Strang,' Jane said. 'But what proof have you that there is a range-war in the offing? My dealings with Mr Gilman were perfectly businesslike. Mr Gilman seems to be a perfectly honest business-man.'

Strang passed a hand over his mouth to hide his wry smile.

'Mr Gilman is a murderin' scoundrel, so is his partner Mr Claybury. If you doubt that, go up to South Dakota an' ask about two brothers who used to own a spread called the Walking W. There are quite a few people yonder who still remember what happened to the Walker brothers an' most of the men who rode for them.'

In the lamplight, the girl's face blanched slightly.

'The Walker brothers! I seem to remember hearing about that. They were murdered weren't they?' The question hung between them for a silent moment then Strang answered with deliberate slowness:

'They were murdered, all right. Seth was shot in the back on a dark night

126

an' Jim was killed by a fellow with a Sharps' buffalo carbine who was planted on top of one of his own barns. Claybury-Gilman was behind the whole deal.'

There was another brief silence during which Jane Tedrow considered the mental pictures of the two killings Strang had mentioned. Out in the bunkhouse, the harmonica player started up with 'Good-bye Old Paint' and the slow music filtered into the house, sounding almost like a dirge. Strang found the eerily appropriate words of one of the verses running through his mind in pace with the music:

*When I die, take my saddle from
   the wall,
Lead my old pony from out of his
   stall;
Tie my bones upon his back, turn
   our faces to the west
An' we'll ride the prairie we love
   the best . . .*

Against the thin wail of the music, Jane asked: 'Why are you bothering to warn me? You have a grudge against Star and Bar and you don't owe me any favours. You pulled me out of that stream. It hurts me to be beholden to you on a further account.'

'I didn't pull you out of that stream to get caught up in the sort of ruckus I think is buildin' up around here, Miss Tedrow,' he told her. 'An' it hurts *me* to think that the Claybury-Gilman bunch probably imagines it has this thing all its own way because it has nothing to fight but a woman an' a bunch of old-timers. Yore riders might have plenty of Rebel fire in them, but you must admit that they aren't so young as they were when they followed the bonny blue flag.'

'Got quite a concern for Star and Bar, considering it pushed your father off that land where you planted your steers, haven't you?' observed the girl. There was no mockery or sarcasm in the remark; rather, there was a note of gratitude. On the heels of the remark, she added: 'There was something I wanted to mention to you. Remember I told you there were things we should talk over?'

Strang nodded, almost enjoying this quiet, lamplit truce that had been established between them.

'It's about that night your father was finally hazed off that land,' she said. 'It wasn't done on my father's orders; in fact, it haunted him for the rest of his days. My father confided things to me in his last illness. He told me about a night the whole outfit rode out to your father's shack. They were drunk after celebrating some Southern anniversary or something. There was something about that night my father never forgot. He told me they trampled around the patches your father had planted and did a good deal of wild shooting, but my father said that, as they rode away, your father called something after him that weighed heavily on him from that moment on. It was something about

Lee and Jackson not approving of his behaviour. It sobered him. My father was a tough pioneer with plenty of rough edges, but he prided himself as an officer of the Confederacy. He never did anything that was unworthy of decent soldierly behaviour, except when he was roaring drunk and that phase of his life came only after the death of my mother and his battle against Cochise and his Apaches for this land.'

Into Strang's mind flooded the memory of the last time he saw Colonel Cal Tedrow. He remembered his slightly hunched figure, sitting his horse and his bearded face touched by the bright crimson brush of the dying sun. He remembered the expression on the old Confederate's face as he glowered back at the nester and his small son, as he had remembered it all these years. Then he said heavily: 'It still didn't stop yore father from chasin' mine off his homestead in the end.'

'That's where you're wrong. It wasn't my father who gunned him off,' she

130

answered. 'It was done by Star and Bar men, but not on my father's orders. What your father said brought mine to thinking how much he had deteriorated since he came to Arizona Territory. The Southern defeat, the fight with the land, the constant attacks by Indians all had a hand in it, but that night at your father's cabin brought him closer to what he had been years before.' Her large eyes wandered to the portrait of the man over the mantel.

'Star and Bar left your father's homestead alone for a long time. Then, one night, some of the boys got tanked up in town and decided they'd have some more fun with the Yankee. So they rode out and chased him off the homestead. They made him saddle up and ride clear off the rangeland on to Skeleton Desert, and they rode after him, shooting off their guns. It wasn't done on my father's orders. It was an independent piece of drunken revelry.'

She fell silent for an instant as memories seeped back to her.

'I was only a little girl at the time, but I remember my father's terrible show of temper when he learned about it. He sent the whole crew out on to the desert to look for your father. They didn't find him. My father was going to make his men apologize to him and bring him back to his homestead. Looking for a single man on that waste of desert is almost impossible and it wasn't until months afterwards that some of our riders discovered his bones and the skeleton of his horse. My father fired every man who had anything to do with hazing your father off his place, but they just wouldn't go, they were too loyal to him. They simply hung around the place like lost boys until he took them on the payroll again.'

Strang said uncomprehendingly: 'You say they found my father's bones! My father didn't die on the desert, he made it to Mexico and died there a short time ago, in bed. Any bones the Star and Bar riders found on Skeleton Desert were somebody else's!'

The girl stared at him for a silent instant in which her face slowly charged with an expression of relief.

'You mean Star and Bar was not responsible for Luke Strang's death?'

Strang gave a negative nod.

'And, all these years, we thought it was. My father died thinking so.'

Strang smiled. 'For someone with a guilty conscience, you didn't do much to make it up to me when I showed up. Runnin' off my cows amounts to rustlin'.' He said it almost chidingly, for a new respect was now established between them. Then, the hard, bitter fact of Nacio Laca's death came to him with the question that was yet to be answered: *was Star and Bar responsible for it?*

Jane Tedrow's face became defiant again.

'What Star and Bar has, it holds,' she told him. 'That was something my father drummed into me. We were here first, and we're staying here!'

'You're goin' to need that fightin'

spirit in spades,' grunted Rod, his voice darkly ominous.

Outside, the harmonica player was still performing in the bunkhouse and above the thin music came the tinkle of ringbits, timed to the clip-clop of a horse. The rider halted and, after a pause, boots and spurs sounded on the gallery outside. Whoever the expected supper guest was, he was familiar enough at the Star and Bar house to dispense with the formality of knocking when he came calling.

He tramped into the house and entered the dining room, but stopped just inside the door, staring in blank surprise at Rod Strang.

And Strang stared back into the dark features of one-armed Marshal Dan Warren!

9

Hostility was undisguised in Dan Warren's eyes. From the door, he glowered at Rod Strang and, when he had put the initial surprise of seeing Strang inside the Star and Bar ranch house behind him, he demanded savagely: 'What are you doin' here?'

Jane Tedrow supplied the answer: 'He's visiting, Dan. He's Rod Strang, the man who put the Running S stock on my land, but he's paying a peaceful visit. In fact, he's just done me a service.'

'I know who he is, we've already met,' the one-armed peace officer almost snarled the words. 'The best service he can do you is to get off yore land. He's one of the trigger-trippers that's floatin' into this country, Jane, but his play is just a little more imaginative than the others' — whatever their game is.'

'You've got it wrong,' Jane told him. 'He's just given me a warning about their game. I think he's honest. He tells me the Claybury-Gilman company is fixing to make a grab for my land because I won't sell out to them.'

For the first time, Rod Strang spoke to the marshal. He retained his relaxed pose in the chair by the table, but there was something in the pose which had the quality of a tightly-wound spring which might fly open at any instant. He spoke quietly, fixing the marshal of San Junipero with bleak eyes.

'She's right, Warren. I'm on the level. I don't know if you've figured out why the gun-totin' saddle-tramps have been showin' here an' there in this country, comin' in easy-like, one at a time, but I have an' it means a grass-war. I saw the Claybury-Gilman bunch prod one along once before.' He paused, as though to allow the languidly spoken words to seep into Dan Warren's brain.

Sitting there with lazy dignity, in spite of his fist-punished features and the scuffed range-garb which showed evidence of the dive he took after her when she was pitched into the stream, Rod Strang took on a curiously noble — and yet potentially dangerous — aspect in Jane Tedrow's eyes. He was looking fixedly at Dan Warren, as if to stare him out of countenance and he spoke his next words as if in studied insult: 'Maybe you do know somethin' about the gunmen you claim to despise, Warren. For all I know, you could be part of their scheme. Certainly you could be a bushwhacker because I know that a left-handed man shot my partner from cover last night then hazed into the brush when I went after him. I wouldn't want to start anythin' under Miss Tedrow's roof, but I aim to kill the man who shot Nacio Laca. You called me in town an' I played too square with you. Next time, I might do the callin' an' I will if I get enough on you for Nacio's murder!'

Warren's handsome face had blanched slightly and he still stood at the door, eyes locked with Strang's.

'You talk foolish, Mister. I didn't kill yore partner,' he said.

'We'll forget it until the settin' is more appropriate to discussin' it,' Strang suggested.

Jane Tedrow looked from one to the other of them with a slightly scowling stony expression. She waved Warren to a vacant chair at the table, then she went into the kitchen to return quickly with a tray bearing full plates of steak and crumbly potatoes.

Marshal Dan Warren's surly face confronted Rod's across the table. This time, *he* was pushing the conversation.

'No, we won't forget it, Strang,' he said tautly. 'I'm interested in this grass-war you claim is comin' up. Where did you see the Claybury-Gilman outfit force this range-war in the past?'

'South Dakota. They up-ended an outfit named the Walkin' W. Ever hear of it?'

Warren blew out his cheeks in a

soundless whistle.

'Who hasn't? It was Lincoln County all over again. But I never heard Claybury an' Gilman were involved,' he murmured.

'They were behind it, pullin' the strings in Chicago. They got trigger-trippers to do their dirty work for big money. They didn't see it as a matter of men an' women, they only see things in terms of longhorns in the Chicago stockyards an' profits on balance sheets.'

Jane Tedrow sat at the end of the table, watching the uneasily matched pair intently and listening acutely to their talk.

'How come you know the back-ground to this Dakota war?' enquired Warren. 'Were you in it?'

'I was on the edge of it. I was marshal of a town called Three Peaks. Just a town marshal with no jurisdiction out-side, but I saw it shape up an' bust wide open from a distance. The situation around here looks too similar for comfort!'

Warren stopped eating for a moment and said: 'I'd like to think you were on the level, then I'd apologize for brawlin' with you this mornin'.'

'An' I'd like to think you didn't kill my partner, then I'd apologize for thinkin' you did.' answered Strang. Each considered the other for a heavy instant then Jane asked: 'What do we do if the Claybury-Gilman company is about to make a fight?'

'Stack this place with ammunition an' pack it with fightin' men. Fort up in here an' be ready to stand 'em off — an', if you ride out, never go alone an' invite 'em to backshoot you. Remember the way things went in the Murphy — Chisum fight in Lincoln County an' the way they're goin' now between the Grahams an' the Tewksburys — everybody layin' up for everyone else an' shootin' like madmen.' Strang spoke quietly and almost philosophically.

'Where do you stand in it?' Warren wanted to know.

140

'I stand alone,' Strang said bluntly and he knew the moment the words left his lips that they were the most empty he had ever uttered in his life. It was impossible to stand alone in a range-war. He had already refused Gilman's offer to join his side as a hired gun — consequently, he had been forced into the Tedrow's camp. It was impossible for him to prowl around these ranges with a lonesome gun, looking out for the land he claimed as his own, while a grass war flared around him. Anyway, he half admitted to himself, he wouldn't be carrying this warning to Jane Tedrow if he wasn't already on Star and Bar's side.

It was a hell of a situation to walk into, he thought savagely. Here he was, sympathizing with the spread that had wronged him in the past, that had set his life savings — in the form of his Running S branded steers — free to go running around over vast tracts of pasture so that he didn't have a hope in the world of catching them . . . that might have murdered his partner. One hell of a situation!

'You can't stand alone with a thing like this shapin' up,' the marshal responded. In the lamplight, his eyes held the beginnings of a new respect for Strang. 'Unless, of course, you aim to clear out of these parts.'

'I don't aim to do that. Got too much of a stake in these parts.'

'Got too much of a likin' for trouble, too. I'd say,' commented Dan Warren. 'Or maybe some people would call it chivalry.'

Rod looked across the table at him sharply and saw that there was nothing mocking in the marshal's face. He figured he could almost like Dan Warren — if he could be sure it wasn't he who shot Nacio Laca.

He finished his meal, waited for Jane and Warren to complete theirs, then stood up, thanking Jane for her hospitality. She eyed him soberly.

'Thanks for bringing the warning,' she said. 'I'll come out with you and one of the boys will bring your pony out of the stable.'

Strang took leave of the marshal curtly and stepped out with Jane. They did not speak as they left the house, nor did anything pass between them save a terse good-bye as he rode out of the yard with his pony trotting behind Nacio's, which he still rode, on a lead rope.

It seemed that the brief truce he had made with Jane Tedrow and Star and Bar was ended.

And in the bunkhouse, the cowhand with the harmonica was playing 'Bury Me Not On The Lone Prairie.'

Strang rode off the Star and Bar headquarters with a turmoil of thoughts tumbling through his head and without knowing where he was going. The closest thing he had to a resting place in this country was the camp he and Nacio had made on the high pastures, but it was only the presence of the cows that made the camp anything like home. Now, they were scattered and mingled far and wide with Jane Tedrow's stock.

To blazes with Jane Tedrow and Star and Bar! He stood alone, looking out for the portion of land he claimed as his own; if there was trouble brewing for Star and Bar, let the outfit stand on its feet and make its own fight. It was nothing to him.

So spoke a fretful voice inside him, but he knew it lied. He knew that things no longer stood between him and Jane Tedrow's outfit the way they stood only a matter of hours ago. What she had told him about her father had been sincere. Old Colonel Tedrow had been willing to leave his father in peace after that night which was graven on Strang's memory. It had not been on Tedrow's orders that Luke Strang had been gunned off his meagre holding.

Strange, thought Strang, but he almost felt he owed it to the old Confederate officer to be around — and on Star and Bar's side — when the devilment that was gathering here to be loosed at his daughter finally burst its bonds.

If only he could be sure that Warren was not responsible for Nacio's killing and that Star and Bar was not mixed up in it, even without Jane's knowledge. He saw that Warren might have holed up and fired on their camp independently of any orders from Star and Bar, but Star and Bar would nevertheless be involved, for Warren might have been protecting the land he planned to marry into one day.

Strang paced the pony easily over tracks of springy grass, leading the animal he had retrieved from the ranch and thinking disjointed thoughts about this land and his future. He'd ridden in here, he and his partner on these self same animals, thinking big thoughts and moulding big schemes. Now, in the space of a few hours, Nacio was under the ground and he was floundering aimlessly on the rim of a grass-war, knowing with a savvy that could not be properly explained that he was going to be involved in it from his bootheels to his ears.

What, he wondered with a cold detachment, was he doing it for?

Marshal Dan Warren had a reason for fighting for this land, even if he was fighting in a dirty fashion; some day, he would settle on it with a wife.

But he, Strang, was pushed by no such prospect. Originally, there was the challenge of fighting for something out of which his father had been cheated, fighting Colonel Cal Tedrow for it. But he had returned to this portion of Arizona to find that boyhood notions do not hold a concrete reality. Old Colonel Tedrow was not the eternal lord of these ranges; he was a mortal man who had died as all mortal men do. And, since that brief talk with Tedrow's daughter in the lamplight of Star and Bar's living room, he had learned that the Colonel was not entirely the ogre he had always imagined him to be. Furthermore, to add to his feeling of deflation, Jane Tedrow, that girl with her mother's loveliness, had exercised her father's doggedness and set his cattle a-wandering.

A shrewd man would have packed his warsack and called it a gamble which had not paid off, but Strang knew he was too stubborn to ride out of here admitting defeat. The memory of Nacio would not allow it until he'd cleared up the matter of his partner's murder. And the storm building up over Star and Bar lands held him with a hypnotic fascination.

He knew he was in this country for keeps, no matter which way the stick floated. He knew he wanted a part of this country.

Arizona was tough and downright cruel in spots, but it had a wide-open bigness and a singular beauty that caught a man and held him. The Territory had put on a brazen pro-Confederate front during the Civil War and it had fought against the depredations of Cochise and his Apaches at the same time. The men who were beginning to call themselves Arizonans had battled against the fanatical Geronimo, who took over where old Cochise left off. They carved out settlements and ranches, watched Geronimo and his yelling braves sweep them into smouldering, corpse-littered rubble, then started building again. They kept building and fighting and Strang knew he was part of their tradition. They would tame this territory of deserts, mesas, canyons and tablelands some day. Some day, Arizona would be respectable; it might even become a state. Strang wanted to be part of it — and he wanted to own a part of it. This part, close to the fringes of the desert, and yet well-watered cattle-raising land.

With a range-war coming on, he thought grimly, he might well wind up part of this land as Nacio Laca was part of it — buried under it!

He rode slowly, gnawing at these thoughts fretfully. Then, it came to him that he was not heading in any particular direction, but trekking aimlessly over the land. He remembered what Jane had told him about the Claybury-Gilman Corporation buying up land bordering Star and Bar's, particularly the Three Sixes land on which were the water-sheds of much of Star and Bar's water. She said that the Three Sixes holdings commenced at Salt Ridge.

Recalling the pattern of the range-war up in South Dakota, which was sparked by the Claybury-Gilman faction damming a stream common to their holdings and those of the Walking W, he felt a strong urge to take a look at the lie of Three Sixes land. He had a vague idea as to where Salt Ridge lay and he pulled his pony and then led the animal about to head in that direction.

Stars twinkled above like jewels set in the vast velvet firmament. There could scarcely have been a more peaceful night since the world was made.

10

A couple of hours of riding under the stars brought Strang to Salt Ridge, a spine of high land jutting up to make a bulwark between Star and Bar's ranges and those of the smaller outfit, the Three Sixes. He crossed the ridge, travelling through a top-land of sparse growths of catclaw and spanish dagger, then angled the two ponies downwards to good salt grass, covering a tableland that unfolded away in the night like a silent sea.

Down at the base of the ridge, he came to a stream and paused to blow his ponies and allow them to drink. It was then, as he was dismounted, waiting for the animals to quit cropping their fill of grass, that he spotted a far point of light. Squinting his eyes in the darkness, he fixed the distant yellow glow, which appeared to be raised some distance above the ground and decided it was not an open fire, but probably the lighted window of a cabin built on some lift of land rising out of the floor of the tableland.

Motivated by a prodding curiosity, he passed up the smoke he was about to roll and mounted again, taking his ponies off in the direction of the distant light. Gradually, it resolved itself into the square of a lighted window.

'Probably a Three Sixes line-camp,' Strang told his mount. And he wondered who could be in the cabin. He recalled that when the Claybury-Gilman outfit bought out the spreads neighbouring the Walker Brothers' Walking W, the old crew were replaced by Claybury-Gilman gunsharps. If the build-up around here was following the same pattern as the Claybury-Gilman move in South Dakota, things would be about the same on the Three Sixes, he mused.

He came near enough to the cabin to see that it was a line-camp shack, clinging to the side of a high hogsback rearing out of the pastureland. There were spindly oaks dotting the lower fringe of the rise and he tethered both ponies to a couple of them, then went up the land towards the yellow glow of the cabin window.

The sharp rasp of harsh laughter and loud talk came from the cabin as he moved towards it. He saw the dark shapes of three horses tethered to a pole hitchrack close to the cabin and he moved in towards the building on a slightly looping course in order to skirt the animals and not alarm them into making a noise. He reached the window from which coppery lamplight bloomed, and flattened himself quickly against the cabin wall so that he could see into the building with a slight twist of his head.

There were three men inside. They were grouped about a table, playing cards. An oil lamp hung from a beam over their heads and it cast a sharply contrasted play of light and shade upon the group.

They all had the stamp of the gun-hung drifter on their garb. There was a tall one who had his back to the window and a black hat cuffed back on his head; a sandy one, shorter than the first, with a sharp nose and a big head, and one younger than his two companions, his tough face crowned with a tight mass of curls which dripped in front of his ears in lank sidewhiskers.

This last of the trio made a triumphant movement with his hand, slapping a card down on the table in answer to one placed there by the tall one whose long back was towards the window.

'Took you that time, Lafe!' guffawed the young man.

The tall man slithered a spur along the boards of the cabin floor in an act of irritation.

'Doggone!' he growled. 'I was plumb sure my luck was in on this game for a change!'

The sandy one grinned across the table amiably and the youngster said: 'Your luck was as much out as it's been all night, Lafe. That's another ten dollars you owe me!'

From his position outside the cabin, Rod Strang studied the back of the tall man with an acute interest. He could not see his face. Only the top of his shoved-back hat and part of his grey-flecked dark hair were visible, but Strang could see that, while the others had shell-belts and holsters draped across the backs of their roughly fashioned chairs, this tall one wore his gun-gear as though he were one of the kind who hated — or were scared — to go without it. He wore a Colt .45. And it was holstered at his left hip.

The tall man shifted uneasily in his chair as Rod watched him.

'I'm cleaned out, Kid,' he complained. 'I'll have to give you an IOU. Gimme a pencil.'

The kid produced a nubbin of pencil and the tall man found a scrap of paper in a shirt pocket. He began to write his gambling debt, holding the pencil in his left hand.

154

'Habitually left handed,' Strang commented to himself. 'It's time for me to call the cards!'

He ducked down to pass under the window, then catfooted around the cabin to its door. He slipped his Colt free of leather, hit the latch of the door, went in quickly and slammed the door behind him, shutting out the star-charmed night and all things save the tense tableau at which he pointed his gun.

The three card-players held stiff poses as if some strange power had petrified them. Still with the pencil in his left hand, the tall man sat arrested in the action of writing, startled eyes fixed on Strang. The kid grasped the edge of the table as if about to jump up but stilled by the sight of the naked gun. The sandy one, whose back was to the door, sat with his head canted about, foxy face bearing an expression of mingled surprise and alarm.

Rod Strang's back was braced hard against the door. The six-shooter was held in an unwavering hand which seemed to cover each of the three men at the table at once.

'It goes off easy,' he warned them. 'Don't give me any cause to use it!'

'What the blazes does this mean?' growled the dark one named Lafe. He was still crouched across the table, his eyes burning on Rod. He had a long-jawed face and a slightly crooked nose. The eyes under his dark tufts of brows were smouldering and dangerous.

'You'll find out,' Strang said. 'I think you're the *hombre* who laid up above my camp an' shot my partner with a Winchester. I should have fixed you in the brush but you hazed out in the darkness. I'll shoot you willingly, so don't present me with an opportunity. You and I are goin' to see a peace officer — you better do as I tell you.'

The tall one remained crouched over the table.

'I don't know what you're talkin' about, Mister,' he objected. His voice had a long-drawn Texas laziness and Rod knew from his manner that he was acting. There was an air of injured innocence to him that was not genuine and it told Strang that he had located the left-handed man who killed Nacio.

Quite suddenly, the tall man uncoiled from his crouching position and came up to his full length, sending his chair skittering from behind his legs. There was murderous intent in his eyes and, blended with the action of springing up, was the blurred dive of his left hand for the .45 at his holster. He was so fast that he had the six-shooter clear of leather and was within a hairsbreadth of triggering it when Strang fired. His Colt bellowed in the close confines of the cabin.

There was a pattern of action which took place within the same instant of time. The tall man stiffened for a moment, as if suddenly frozen solid; in the same instant, the kid was clawing for the gun and shell-belt which was slung across the back of his chair and the sandy, sharpfaced one scooted across the cabin to hold a terrified pose against one wall.

Then, the tall one dropped his gun. There was an exaggerated screwed-up expression on his face like that of one who had just tasted an extra bitter lemon. He fell face down across the table as heavily as a sack of sand.

The kid was on his feet, dancing backwards with his gun out of leather, a savage grin drawing back his mouth. From the door, Strang fired low deliberately, turning the youngster's grin into a twisted grimace of anguish. He dropped his six-shooter and grabbed at his left leg with a howl. Abruptly, he was off balance, staggering backwards, and he sat down suddenly on the scarred boards of the floor, nursing his leg and whimpering faintly.

Through flat wreaths of cordite smoke, Strang turned his attention to the sandy one. There was no opposition from him. He was flattened against the wall, eyes round as coins and a look of shocked alarm on his face. There was a silent moment of anti-climax, heavy with the stink of gunsmoke, then Rod stepped forward, and kicked the kid's fallen gun out of the youngster's reach. The kid began to gasp with pain again and the sandy one simply stood against the wall, gripped by fear.

'You busted my leg!' complained the youngster almost indignantly.

'I warned you not to attempt anythin',' Strang said coldly. He nodded towards the corpse on the table. 'What's his name?'

'Lafe Alford.' The answer came from the sandy one.

'I've heard of him. Texas gunfighter. Pretty fast, and pretty cowardly,' Strang murmured. 'Why did he hole up an' make a partially successful bushwhack attempt on my camp?'

'I don't know. Me an' Kid just arrived here today. We don't know anythin' about what Lafe's been doin'.'

'Just arrived from where?'

'Utah.'

'Came from Utah because you heard the Claybury-Gilman bunch was offerin' trigger-wages, huh?' asked Strang stonily. 'How many more rannihans have they taken on the payroll?'

From the floor, the kid complained: 'My leg's givin' me hell, Mister! Gimme a hand up to that chair!'

Strang ignored him.

'How many more gunslicks have they brought into this country?'·he pressed.

'I don't know,' whined the sandy man. 'We just arrived. We don't know anythin' about the set-up.'

'This spread is packed with gunnies, ain't it?' Strang asked. 'There ain't a decent cowpoke on the outfit. They were fired or they rode off quietly when the Claybury-Gilman company took over. An' it's the same with the Box Triangle an' the Lazy K. There are scum of yore kind on three sides of Star and Bar grass. You figure it's goin' to be a tolerably easy grab; there's nothin' to fight but a woman an' a bunch of worn-out oldsters.'

160

'Gimme a hand up to the chair,' howled the youngster from the floor. His face was ashen and he was in obvious pain. Strang turned his attention to the kid.

'What were you planted up here in this old line-camp for?' he enquired. 'Because you can see over Salt Ridge an' look down on Star and Bar land from here an' spot any riders who might come investigatin' after you Claybury-Gilman toughs have made the usual Claybury-Gilman openin' gambit of dammin' up common water so it can't reach Star and Bar?'

The injured youngster shot him a glance which told him he had approached the truth and Strang grunted with a species of satisfaction. The same pattern he had known in South Dakota was being worked out here in Arizona.

Strang motioned to the sandy one with his six-gun.

'Help him up into that chair. Then take his shell-belt off, put his gun on the table an' tie his hands behind his back with the belt,' he ordered. He added a caution: 'Don't be tempted to try anythin' while you have the gun in yore hand or I'll drop you.'

The sharp featured sandy man complied with the order. With the kid's gun on the table, he fastened the kid's hands at the back of the chair. The kid allowed him to do it without complaint, save for an occasional moan of pain.

'Now put yore own belt an' gun on the table an' tote Lafe down the rise an' put him across the led pony I have down there,' Strang said.

The sandy one hefted up the dead weight of Lafe Alford with considerable difficulty and slowly carried him out of the door which Strang held open. Strang walked after him, still with a naked gun, directing the sandy man down the darkened rise. With a grunt, the sandy one slung the corpse over the saddle-less back of the pony at the end of the lead rope and stood for a moment catching his breath.

For an instant, he seemed to find

some measure of courage.

'Damnedest fellow I ever met, *hombre*,' he grumbled. 'You came here to kill a man an' brought a led pony to tote his body away. Who are you, anyway?'

'None of your concern,' drawled Strang, waving impatiently with his gun. 'Just you walk back to the cabin.' They went back to the line-camp shack, Strang still covering the sandy man.

In the cabin, the kid began to complain, in obvious pain.

'Darn you, Mister, you ain't goin' to leave me here with a busted leg, are you?' he pleaded. 'It's beginnin' to hurt like blazes!'

'That's too bad,' sympathized Strang. 'But you came into this country to make trouble an' trouble caught up with you first. I ain't aimin' to leave you alone, you'll have a companion an' pretty soon. I figure some of yore Claybury-Gilman friends will be along to give you a helpin' hand. I'll give you both some advice an' you can pass it on to the rest of your gunslick friends. Get out of this country — this is one grass-war that ain't goin' to be so easy. There'll be more of you in the same condition as Lafe Alford, an' you can tell that to Mr Claybury an' Mr Gilman if you happen to meet them.'

Rod gave the sandy man an unceremonious push that sent him into one of the chairs, then he tied his hands behind his back with his own shell-belt in the same way that the kid was trussed. He checked the security of the kid's bonds, emptied the chambers of the two six-shooters on the table, meticulously slipped the shells out of the loops in the belts binding the pair to their chairs and dropped them into his shirt pocket.

He gave them a curt good night and walked out into the night breeze. Wearily, for he was beginning to feel the strain of an eventful day, he made his long-legged way down the hump to where the ponies were tethered. There was a little elation in his heart. At least, he reflected, he had found the left handed man who had shot Nacio Laca. Lafe Alford had shown guilt in his face when challenged — and he had been rash enough to attempt to draw and shoot it out with the man he had not succeeded in killing when he fired his Winchester from the shelter of the rock on the high pastures. Strang reflected, too, that he owed that fighting wildcat of a marshal in San Junipero an apology, but he'd get around to that soon enough.

He clambered into his saddle and made a couple of hours' steady riding, leading the spare pony with Alford's corpse draped limply across it. He rode off the Three Sixes, heading in the general direction of San Junipero, traversing part of the Star and Bar holdings.

Dawn was broadening in the sky when he reached a stand of trees clustered about a small stream. He dismounted, allowed the ponies to drink, then settled under a tree with his hat pulled over his eyes. The last thing he remembered before he fell asleep was that a couple of bright and early jackrabbits were eyeing him from behind a tree bole with nervous curiosity.

11

One-handed, Marshal Dan Warren rolled a Bull Durham smoke as he leaned against a post on the gallery of his office. He was watching the single street of San Junipero with a slit-eyed vigilance that was second nature to him, although it was early and the town was not yet fully awake.

It was a little after seven and the sun was already flooding the town with its brassy brilliance. Warren had eaten his breakfast, as was his custom, at the Calton's eating house and ambled back to his office at the rear of which he had his bachelor's living quarters. His daily round as marshal of San Junipero had started early that day, for a horseman, bearing an envelope from the nearest railhead at Gila Junction, had called at the office almost as soon as Warren returned from his meal.

Warren was surveying the street languidly, looking for nothing in particular and all things in general. His mind was concerned with the ominous situation shaping up in this country. There had been a steady arrival of obvious border riff-raff during the last few weeks. Men of the gunpacking variety were seen briefly around the town, then they disappeared. Other individuals of the same gunslinger stamp passed through San Junipero while Warren was still trying to memorise the faces of the first transient rannihans. Wherever they went to, these birds of passage, Warren was pretty sure they did not leave the vicinity. They were here looking for pickings of some kind, he was sure. And now, Rod Strang, the tough rider who had come to make a private war upon Star and Bar, had supplied the answer. They came into the San Junipero country and holed up on the spreads owned by the Claybury-Gilman combine, the spreads which bordered Star and Bar.

The Claybury-Gilman outfit was paying these gunnies trigger-wages.

Warren harboured a new respect for Strang since their talk in the lamplight at the Star and Bar ranch house the previous night and that respect had been intensified since the rider from Gila Junction arrived with the envelope a short time before.

The marshal blew out a string of smoke to deter an ambitious mosquito from making a landing on his nose. He put a certain venom into the action.

It was a pity, he told himself, that he was not as wise as he was at this moment when that plausible, smooth-talking businessman from Chicago was in San Junipero to talk terms with Jane Tedrow. But he knew he had become wise too late. Amos Gilman had left the previous day to take a train at Tucson which would ultimately take him back to Chicago. But he knew that Gilman had left orders hereabouts. Orders prompted by Jane's continued refusal to sell out. Orders to make war.

Out on the street, people were beginning to show themselves. Storekeepers were sweeping the plankwalks in front of their establishments; an ore wagon which was used as a supply vehicle for the miners out at the Jubilation Mine rolled up to collect stores, its driver half asleep behind the team of long-eared mules, and the sultry desert breeze carried the ring of hammer against anvil from the high structure of Dick McCarthy's blacksmith shop.

Dan Warren took a new interest in the street when he saw a familiar rider approaching, pacing his pony over the ruts at an unhurried gait and leading a second animal. The few citizens on the boardwalks stopped to stare at the rider and the burden carried by the led pony.

Across its back was a dead man whose hanging arms and legs swung slackly to the movement of the pony.

The one-armed marshal pitched his spent smoke off the gallery and stood watching Rod Strang approach the law office with his grisly burden. Strang still had grimed strips of court plaster on his face and he bore the plum coloured bruises of the beating the marshal had given him the previous day. He needed a shave badly and the stubble and caked alkali dust on his face gave him a curiously artificial expression of ferocity. Like that of an Apache wearing war-paint, thought Warren.

The peace-officer watched the approach of Strang and his burden, noted that he was headed directly for the marshal's office and called: 'Are you bringin' that here?'

A small crowd of townsfolk was gathering along the street, watching the progress of Strang with interest. Because of these spectators, Strang chose not to answer the marshal until he hauled his rein at the gallery of the marshal's office.

He swung out of the saddle, mounted the gallery and said: 'He's the fellow who bushwhacked my partner. I met up with him on Three Sixes land last night an' was fixin' to bring him to you alive, but he hauled his iron on me. It was him or me. I had my gun on him when he slapped leather but he probably figured I'd hesitate to shoot. He figured wrong. His name's Lafe Alford an' he's a second-rate Texas gunman.'

'I've heard of him,' nodded Warren. He stepped off the gallery and walked over to the led pony to examine the corpse of Alford. He strode back to Strang.

'Wears his gun on his left. That the only proof you have that he was the man who shot yore partner?' he asked.

'He was left handed in everything. His guilt showed on his face when I mentioned Nacio's killing an' he underlined it when he made a snatch for his gun when I told him I was bringin' him to you.'

'Last time I heard of Alford, there was a couple of hundred dollars on his head for some shootin' he did some-where,' mentioned Warren. 'Did you bring him here to claim the bounty?'

'Not particularly. I brought him here by way of provin' my contention that the Claybury-Gilman outfit is movin' in with gunfighters of Alford's kind. There are a couple more up in a line-shack on the Three Sixes spread. It looks right down on Star and Bar land; that's why these guys were planted there. There are others planted at strategic points on the Lazy K land, too, or I miss my guess.' Strang paused for a moment and eyed the marshal squarely. 'I also rode into town to make you an apology,' he said. 'I said I'd apologize for thinkin' you were a back-shooter if I was sure you didn't kill Nacio. Now, I know you didn't and I'm offerin' you that apology.'

Marshal Dan Warren studied the punished boarding of the gallery floor for a moment.

'You don't have to make any apologies,' he said slowly. He jerked his head towards the pony and its limply hanging burden out on the street. 'We'll lay Alford out in the stable at the back of the office, then I'll arrange for his burial. He'll get six feet by three up on Graveyard Hill, then I'll have to make out a report an' take some details from you. There isn't a coroner nearer than Tombstone an' we can't leave him unburied until the coroner gets over here for an inquest.'

Strang and the marshal walked the ponies around the rear of the office, spread Alford on clean straw and covered him with a tarp. They trudged back to the front to enter the office and, as they passed through the portals, the one-armed marshal said, with a philosophic note in his voice: 'Could be there'll be inquests a-plenty for the coroner when he finally does get over this direction, the way things are shapin' up hereabouts.'

Rod said nothing, but dropped wearily into a chair close to the marshal's spur-scarred desk. After the mounting heat of the street, the interior of the office was comparatively cool. It was orderly for a place of its kind.

There were half a dozen carbines for the use of deputies locked in a rack against one wall and the bold-lettered reward dodgers put out by Wells-Fargo and other stage lines were tacked on the wall above the rack.

Dan Warren pitched his hat on to his desk and reached for an open envelope. He slid a folded paper out of it and Strang saw that it was a wire. Warren handed it to him.

'No, you don't owe me any apologies,' he said, picking up the thread of their earlier conversation. 'I should apologize to you. And I do apologize for thinkin' you were just another of the gun-packin' gentry that's been floatin' into these parts of late, an' for sailin' into you the way I did yesterday. I promised myself I'd beat the daylights out of the next gunnie who came to San Junipero an' you just happened to look the part. After I left the Star and Bar house last night, I rode over to the telegraph at Gila Junction to send a wire to Three Peaks, rememberin' what you'd told me. That's the answer, it came this mornin'.'

Rod was already reading the tersely worded wire:

'Rod Strang elected and served term of office as US Marshal in this city three years ago. Carried out duties with highest efficiency and devotion. To our regret declined to run for further term.

George A. Seligman, Mayor, Three Peaks, South Dakota.'

The marshal of San Junipero stretched out his single hand. Rod shook it gravely.

'Looks like we make common cause. Let's forget the past,' suggested Warren.

'All right. We'll forget some of it at least, but I'm still aimin' to take the land I claim is mine — even though I'm with Star and Bar in whatever ruckus the Claybury-Gilman bunch is cookin' up.' Strang cautioned.

Dan Warren gave a wry smile. 'Pretty

stubborn galoot, ain't you?'

'That's been said before. I'm pretty stubborn, all right. There are times when a man has to be.'

'I know it.' answered the marshal. 'I'm tolerably stubborn myself.'

'An' a tolerably hard hitter,' grunted Strang, rubbing his bruised features. 'Any place around here where I can clean up?'

'In my room at the back. You can heat water on the stove an' borrow my razor,' Warren said. 'Then I recommend breakfast at the Sunset. Ruthie has surpassed herself this mornin'. She's made flapjacks. They're too good to miss.'

'Yeah, I was contemplatin' breakfastin' over there.'

'I figured you might be,' returned Dan Warren with a knowing nod. 'That's why I suggested the razor.'

Rod grinned. A mighty likeable *hombre*, this one-time cavalry sergeant, he thought, mighty likeable now that one knew he was a square shooter and not a bushwhacker.

He washed and shaved, borrowed a comb and tamed his dark hair. He slapped the dust from his clothing and sombrero then strolled across the street to the Sunset Eating House.

The last of the breakfast customers were leaving as he made his way up to the counter. Ruth Calton, looking cool and efficient as ever, was giving change to a customer who had just paid for his meal. Strang waited until she had finished, then asked: 'Any of those flapjacks left?'

The girl with the night-black hair turned and saw him for the first time. Her face showed pleasure.

'There are some left,' she informed him. 'Take a seat.'

Rod established himself at one of the tables in the now empty eating house. Ruth went into the kitchen and returned with a tray on which there was a heaped plate of flapjacks and a pot of coffee. Strang made a start on the breakfast and found that Warren was right in his contention that Ruth's cooking that morning was too good to miss.

Ruth busied herself behind the counter, allowing him to eat in quiet. When he had finished and was touching a match to a newly rolled cigarette, she came across the room and sat at the table with him.

Her face was grave, but she disguised its gravity briefly by smiling and asking: 'Did I detect a more friendly note in your meeting with the marshal this morning?'

'You must have been spying out of the window,' accused Rod and he felt mildly flattered when he saw a flush of bashfulness touch her cheeks and cause her to look away suddenly.

Doggone, he thought with something close to astonishment, *this girl has it bad on my account! She must have been peekin' at me from the window.* Then he recalled that he had taken special care with his toilet in the marshal's living quarters before coming over here and a slight flush mounted his own cheeks.

He took up the thread of the conversation and told her: 'The marshal's all right. A mighty friendly fellow when you meet him on the right terms.'

'I told you he was,' she said sagely. Then she asked: 'Who was that dead man you brought into town?'

'A man who came into this country to make trouble,' Rod said.

'You shot him, didn't you?'

'Yeah, because he would have shot me if I didn't.'

The troubled expression clouded her darkly haloed face again.

'It's all part of the ugly business that's shaping up around here, isn't it?' she asked. 'The ugly business Dan Warren felt was coming up when those shady gun carriers began to appear in this country.'

Rod nodded. 'I'm afraid it is. There's a storm about to break in this locality an' there's no point in my denyin' it.'

'An' those thievin' Claybury-Gilman people are behind the storm, ain't they?' demanded the voice of George Calton.

Strang and the girl turned to see that Calton had come up to the table unknown to them. He was cold sober and his face was set in hard lines. 'I heard you talkin' to Gilman in Bannock's saloon yesterday, young fellow,' he went on. 'That Claybury-Gilman bunch squeezed me off my ranch by sharp business methods. I guess I was too unimportant for them to make a full scale war against me, they just used their various catspaws to push me out of the market after a couple of miserable seasons in which I lost a lot of stock. I'll tell you one thing, young man: if there's a fight comin' up against the Claybury-Gilman crew, I aim to have a part of it!'

'*Father!*' objected Ruth. 'You're talking nonsense!'

'No. I ain't. I have a score against the Claybury-Gilman combine. It's the one thing I want to see settled more than anythin' else.'

'I understand what your father means, Ruth,' Strang said quietly. 'Sometimes a man can take a powerful amount of kickin' around, but there comes a time when he has to start kickin' back. If he doesn't, his self respect just drifts away. Mostly, a man doesn't much care what others think of him, but when he starts to think of himself as a worthless piece of human furniture on the scene, he's through.'

George Calton drew up his long body to its impressive height. He looked a lot less the town drunk and much more a fighting cowman.

'He understands, all right, Ruth,' he told his daughter.

Turning to Strang, he stipulated: 'Remember young fellow, if a fight comes up around here, I'm gettin' in it!'

12

Dan Warren dropped his pen on his desk having completed his report on the death of Lafe Alford. Bright sunlight streamed into his office and put a golden patina on his face.

He asked the question that had been hanging between Strang and himself since their meeting the previous night. 'How soon do you figure they'll make their fight against Star and Bar?'

Across the desk, Rod Strang shrugged.

'No tellin'. Maybe they'll play it slowly an' squeeze Star and Bar by damming their water an' makin' the stock suffer — on the other hand, maybe my tangle with the fellows in the lion-camp shack will prod them into somethin' more hasty.'

'That's what I was figurin',' the Marshal replied. 'When I was at the ranch last night, I took stock of the weapons there. They have a pretty strong arsenal an' every man jack on the place is ready to defend it. I told them to fort up the house an' gather every slug they could lay their hands on — but I still figure they'll need more ammunition. There's ammunition a-plenty at Eldon's store here in town. I suggest we take possession of it before the other side does an' get it out to Star and Bar as quickly as we can.'

Strang nodded. 'Seems a sensible thing to do. You aimin' to leave the town without a marshal while you get in on this fight?'

'I have a deputy, Dick Flinders. He's in bed over at the boardin' house where he lives right now. He was on duty last night. I'm turnin' the town over to him an' I'm fightin' this thing as a private citizen, not as town marshal. After all, I have some stake in Star an' Bar grass — at least, I hope to have some day.'

Rod offered him a tough grin. 'Yeah,' he commented slowly, 'so have I!' He tilted back his chair to a position which allowed him to look out of the open door into the sun-splashed street as he reached for the makings of a cigarette. His hand stilled at his shirt pocket with the tobacco sack half out of his pocket. The jingle of ringbits and the brisk pounding of hoofs came from the street.

'Three *hombres* comin' here!' Strang said. 'Look like gunnies to me!'

The marshal stood up and looked out of the window positioned at one side of his desk. He saw three big-hatted, tough featured riders pulling rein outside the office and wheeling their animals around so that they faced the gallery. Slowly, he strode out on to the gallery.

'You stay here,' he ordered Strang. 'But come out smokin' if there's any call to.'

The riders were positioned in line, facing the gallery. They sat their saddles with a calculated insolence, bodies canted slightly forward in the leather and hands crossed on their saddle-horns. They had the mark of the gunman branded on them. Six-shooters sprouted at their thighs and carbines were sheathed at their saddles.

The man in the centre, who wore a faded blue shirt, a dun hide vest and a flat-crowned hat, was apparently the spokesman. He considered the marshal in an unhurried fashion, his eyes dark slits in a thin, long-jawed face. The three horses pawed uneasily at the dust of the street and swished at annoying flies with their tails.

'We've come for the body of Alford,' stated the middle horseman.

'Who are you?' demanded Warren easily.

'Hands from the Three Sixes,' said the middle man. 'We heard that the man who murdered Alford brought him here an' we've come for him.'

'Yeah, an' we've come for the feller who killed him, too,' rasped the rider at the spokesman's left, his comment ending in a slight giggle. The spokesman whirled his head about quickly to scowl at the man on his right by way of telling him to shut up. Warren considered the one with the giggle. He was lean and long-nosed with a nervous habit of twitching his shoulders. His eyes smouldered under the shade of his dusty sombrero. The giggle seemed to be on the point of bubbling from his thick lips even as the spokesman glowered at him.

He was either a touch demented or a mite drunk, thought Warren.

'You ain't any Three Sixes hands that I ever knew,' commented Dan Warren casually.

'We're new riders,' the middle horseman said. 'The old ones got disillusioned an' travelled on — they got dissatisfied about pay or somethin'.'

Warren leaned the stump of his amputated arm against a gallery post, his hand hanging close to his thonged down holster. He held a deceptively easy pose there and chatted to the middle horseman as casually as if they were old friends passing the time of day at a street corner.

'Well now, it seems to me that you ain't so much new hands at the Three Sixes as hired gunslicks, brought into this country to do a chore that decent hands wouldn't do,' he said. 'Seems to me that was why Alford was in this country, too. He had a price on his head, a small one, I grant you, but it's my guess that you galoots haven't even got that kind of price on yore heads. In other words, you're even more worthless than Lafe Alford.'

'You ain't got a very pleasant way of jokin', Marshal,' objected the middle rider. 'We came in here to claim the body of a fellow hand, not to be insulted.'

Dan Warren lost none of his easy manner.

'You came in here to make trouble,' he contradicted pleasantly. 'You came here for the body of Alford, sure, because Alford is a known criminal an' yore employers don't want it generally known that they plant his kind on isolated line-camps to spy on other people's land. You also came to fix the man who fixed Alford. You ain't gettin' Alford's corpse, an' you ain't getting the man who shot him.'

In the office, Rod sat tilted in the chair. He could see the halted riders beyond the gallery rail and they could see him. He admired Warren's cool manner but he knew the marshal was pushing a fight in that peculiar way of prodding for trouble that Ruth Calton had said was due to the fact that he figured he was living on borrowed time. Strange way for a man to behave when he was contemplating marriage, thought Strang.

The three horses shifted uncomfortably in the blazing sun, kicking at the dust fractiously and swiping at flies with their tails. In their saddles, the riders were easing themselves slowly into positions which made for the more facile drawing of six-shooters.

'You ain't a very friendly person,' complained the centre rider pettishly. 'It's fellows like you that make other fellows do things they don't really want to do, Marshal.'

'Things like shootin' marshals?' prodded Warren with his tantalizingly pleasant manner.

Strang came up from his chair lazily and strode across to the door of the marshal's office. He stood in the door with a languid attitude matching that of Dan Warren out on the gallery. He took in the mounted trio with cold, gunfighter's perception. There was the centre man, tall in the saddle with a long-jawed face; there was the lean one with the dangerously smouldering eyes and the twitch to his narrow shoulders and there was the third rider, stocky, heavily built and with a sunburned, tight-lipped grizzled face.

They had the look of bullet-throwing border scum stamped all over them — and Warren was prodding them.

'Well, I asked you — do you feel like shootin' yourself a marshal today?' continued Warren and Strang remembered the way he had started to push him towards grabbing his gun when they first met. The marshal of San Junipero was convinced that he could outdraw Strang, otherwise he wouldn't have pushed the issue. And he was convinced he would come off best in a pistol showdown with these three ruffians, or he would not be bulldogging them this way.

It occurred to Rod that he had never seen the marshal draw with that single hand of his — maybe he *was* good. A man would have to be good to go looking for bullet trouble with gun-heavy rannihans the way he did!

The man in the centre of the lined-up group of Three Sixes horsemen considered Dan Warren for a minute in which bayonet points of hard light showed in his eyes. The minute extended like a wet rawhide thong being drawn taut, then it snapped against the sultry air of the sunpunished street with the sharp, hissing rasp of the centre horseman's voice as he snarled:

'Ain't no damned one-winged badge

toter goin' to get *gay with me!*'

He pitched his right hand down for his holstered six-gun and the men saddled on either side of him did the same as if activated by a single string. But as the centre man clawed for his iron with his right hand, his left was thrown up in what seemed to be a brief, imperative signal.

Strang bounced out of the marshal's office, his unsheathed gun in his hand. Even as he went, he saw several fragments of action as a series of disconnected pictures, as he had often done in the past when involved in gunfights.

He saw Warren draw his six-shooter in the swiftest, blurring action he had ever seen; the middle rider was suddenly twisting backwards in his saddle, flinging his gun away from him as Warren's pistol slammed a deafening explosion across the gallery and Warren was abruptly dancing into a low crouch, ducking a badly aimed bullet from the gun of the lean man with twitching shoulders as he tried to fire and control his scared and prancing mount at the same time. The third rider was too busy fighting to control his jittery horse to shoot, but the awareness that the lean one's shoulders were given a final twitch as Warren's gun blasted a second time scared him visibly. His sun-peeled face turned a sickly yellow and he yanked his horse about to hightail up the street.

But behind all this action which had bellowed into life as Rod Strang stood with a still cold gun, there was the grim answer to the hand signal the central Three Sixes rider had given the moment he clawed for his iron.

Hostile riders were coming down the street, pounding directly for the marshal's office in rising blossoms of dust. They had issued from the cross alleys between the adobe and timber structures of stores and saloons.

There were eight of them.

They had entered town by riding along the rear alleys which ran behind

the buildings and they had posted a
sentinel at the opening of one of the
cross alleys to watch for the signal
which would be given by the spokesman who spoke to the marshal. This
was not an instance of three riders
coming into the town to make wild
trouble. It was a big scale arrival of
gunslingers bent on hot lead business
and that business was to wipe out two
factors hostile to the plan of the
Claybury-Gilman faction in its bid for
the Star and Bar grass. The factors were
Marshal Dan Warren and Rod Strang,
two men with gun savvy whose
sympathies lay with Jane Tedrow's
outfit!

'*Trouble!*' crisped Warren urgently.
'*Get doggo on the gallery, they'll start
shootin' any minute!*'

Strang was down already, pressing his
flat-muscled stomach to the rough
flooring of the gallery, levelling his Colt
through the railings. Warren was beside
him and the group of furiously
pounding riders, joined by the rider

who had been scared yellow and who seemed now to have found courage in numbers, were charging down the street in an attack on the marshal's office.

The two horses on which sagged the rannihans Warren had shot, had cantered off, panicky at the thunder of gunfire.

'Give me your gun,' said Warren calmly. 'I'm two shells short.'

He slid his own Colt across the gallery floor to Strang who quickly saw the logic of this move. In killing the two Three Sixes ruffians, he had used two shells, but his disability meant he could not push shells from his belt-loop into the empty chambers quickly. But Strang's gun was unfired with its chambers full. Strang, with the advantage of two hands, thumbed two shells into the empty chambers of the exchanged gun. He was just in the narrow nick of time — but the pair flattened on the gallery of the law office met the charging gunslingers with fully loaded six-shooters.

The Three Sixes bunch came level with the gallery, churning up banners of dust so that the horses and riders looked like fast-moving, hazy phantoms. A fusillade of shots cracked from the mass of pounding riders and slugs whined and screamed around the gallery. Shards of sundried wood were torn from the gallery and hot lead thumped into the powdery adobe of the building.

Strang and Warren fired almost lazily, each marking a man, disregarding the whining leaden hornets which zipped angrily around their flattened bodies. One of the attackers dropped out of his saddle as Strang's gun exploded and a second followed him as Warren fired. The attackers had passed the office and their broadside had been ineffective. They had not yet marked the positions of the two men flattened on the gallery to hit them with shots fired as they rode by at speed, but they were wheeling their animals now, making ready for a second dash past the marshal's office.

Strang glared through the interstices of the gallery rail and saw them yanking leather to pull their mounts around. They flourished their guns in urgent gestures, each rallying the other to a second outburst of shooting. Then they were coming back along the street in a hoof-pounding knot, their teeth showing white in vindictive grins as they churned up sun-touched dust.

'Here they come again,' commented Dan Warren casually, and Rod had time to reflect that he was being given a glimpse of the kind of cool courage that a certain wounded cavalry sergeant had shown in getting his men clear of the Dragoon mountains when Geronimo's Apaches had worked them over — then he was shooting again, blasting into the mob of riders for all he was worth. The Three Sixes men were level with the gallery now and they were smoking it out in a fury of slamming guns, rising dust, stinking cordite and whining slugs. Some of the bolder spirits had actually halted their animals in a determined attempt to hit the pair who made so difficult a target by lying flat behind the gallery railings.

Slugs spanged around the front of the marshal's office viciously, Warren's hat went spinning from his head and a bullet ripped a wooden interstice near enough Rod's head to shower it with splinters.

The pair on the gallery dropped a couple of the raiders, then Warren's gun clicked empty. Strang cursed as he fired at a raider, missed him as the man lunged to one side on a panicky horse. Then his own six-shooter clicked futilely as the pin struck on an empty chamber.

From the midst of the milling knot of horses fronting the gallery in a deter-mined stand, guns bellowed remorselessly and the raiders' bullets were less wildly hurled. The adobe wall backing Strang and Warren was pitted and slugs were tearing into the rails of the gallery and its wooden flooring.

Strang and Warren pressed themselves hard against the boards. Cornered with empty guns and little opportunity to reload in this bullet-bitten uproar, it looked as though the two who prided themselves on their gun savvy had put themselves into a gun trap from which they could never escape.

Then, in the midst of the crashing guns, the whinnying of horses and the hammering of hoofs, there came a new note — the carefully spaced roar of a carbine. The men on the gallery saw one of the raiders drop his six-gun and grab at his shoulder; a horse went down under another rider. Suddenly, the remainder of the raiding party was hazing up the street in retreat. Where there had been nine, only four were left. Three rode away at a panicky clip, one of them sagging in his saddle and clutching at his shoulder while the fourth, who had been unhorsed, was busily mounting the animal of a dead rider. He, too, hazed after his companions and the mysterious Winchester spoke behind them, not hitting them, but bellowing with a steady precision to send fountains of dust spurting out of the ground in the wake of the fleeing gunnies.

Strang turned a sweat streaked face to Warren who was blowing out his cheeks in a sigh of relief.

'Where's that *hombre* with the Winchester?' demanded Strang, slitting his eyes to peer through the thick wreaths of cordite smoke which fogged the gallery.

'Take a look across the street,' indicated Warren. 'Right on top of the Sunset Eatin' House. There's the man who saved our bacon.'

Strang squinted across the street and upwards. He saw the sun touching a bright glitter to a Winchester barrel and he saw that the man who gripped it, lying on the roof of the eating house with his head and shoulders protruding over the edge, was George Calton.

Strang and Warren came up from the gallery floor and dusted themselves down. Out on the street, the dead raiders were stretched in the dust and a couple of loose horses pranced around fractiously. Citizens who had bolted for cover when the shooting began were showing their noses with caution.

The marshal and Strang exchanged guns so that each had his own again.

'We make a pretty good team, you an' me,' stated Warren drily. 'But we had ourselves in a hole until George opened up.'

'Yeah. But with George along, I'd say we make a mighty good team,' Strang answered.

A wild-eyed and wild-haired young man, hatless and wearing a deputy marshal's badge, came running up to the gallery.

'What's been goin' on, Dan?' he demanded. 'I was sound asleep at the boardin' house then I heard shootin'. I no sooner fell into my duds an' got my shell belt on than the whole thing was over!'

'Just some gentlemen decided to look us up, Dick,' Warren told him. 'Meet Rod Strang, a man about whom you an' me have had the wrong idea. Mr Strang an' I stood 'em off for a time, but the fact that we didn't get ourselves drilled in the end is due to Mr Calton who is now appearin' behind you.'

Deputy Marshal Dick Flinders turned around to see the lean frame of George Calton, the town drunk, mounting the gallery steps. Calton carried a Winchester, looked as sober as a judge and very well pleased with himself.

'Mighty good while it lasted,' commented Calton, nodding to Warren and Strang. 'I got a tolerable amount of pleasure out of that little ruckus.'

'An' we got a tolerable amount of relief out of seein' you show up on the roof, George,' Warren said. 'Come into the office. I have a bottle of good whiskey in my desk. We're all goin' to have a drink.'

George Calton shook his head gravely.

'No,' he declared firmly. 'I'm off that stuff for good!'

And they could see he meant it.

13

The corpses of the raiders had joined that of Lafe Alford in the stable at the rear of the marshal's office which had been left in the care of Deputy Dick Flinders, and three men, Strang, Warren and George Calton, were mounted up in front of the office. Across the saddle-horn of the marshal's horse was slung a gunny sack containing ammunition from Eldon's store.

They were making ready to ride out to the Star and Bar headquarters. Warren and Strang had worked out the meaning of the arrival of the Three Sixes raiders in San Junipero. The men could only have arrived because the pair which Strang had trussed up in the line cabin had been discovered by their fellow Three Sixes riders and the coming of the Claybury-Gilman bunch to San Junipero was their means of disposing of two formidable fighting men whose sympathies lay with Star and Bar.

It had failed, but it had marked the breaking of the storm which had been building up over these ranges for weeks. That storm must eventually wreak its full wrath on the coveted Star and Bar spread and the marshal, with the fighting man who had once declared himself to be a lone wolf, chasing his own interests in the Star and Bar vicinity, was riding out to help with the defence of the ranch. With them rode Calton, sometime town drunk of San Junipero, but now a man who had found his courage and who was itching for another opportunity to mix it with the Claybury-Gilman organization.

Calton sat his saddle grim featured. He wore faded dungarees and his floppy brimmed hat and he nursed his Winchester across his saddle pommel. The whole town knew George Calton best as a human appendage to one or the other of the bars in which cowhands and miners swilled away their earnings, but there was not a man in San Junipero who saw him astride his borrowed horse that morning who failed to see in him a determined fighting man.

Ruth Calton came out of the eating house, crossed the street hurriedly, holding the skirts of her neat dress clear of the fouled and hoof-pounded dirt. She stopped in the midst of the mounted men, looking earnestly at her father.

'Not goin' to try stoppin' him, are you?' asked Rod.

Ruth shook her head.

'No. I don't want to see him get hurt, but I wouldn't try to stop him after what you said about a man sometimes having to fight for his self respect. My father's always been proud of being a cowman; this is a cowman's fight and I can see he belongs in it!'

George Calton grinned at his daughter's words.

'Hear that, you *hombres?*' he asked

his two companions. 'That's a cow-man's daughter talkin'.'

Marshal Dan Warren gave Ruth Calton a tough grin.

'I'm glad you don't object, Ruthie,' he said. 'Gettin' in this fight means quite a lot to yore father — an' he'll mean a lot to us now that we've seen how he uses a Winchester. We better move; we'll have to get this ammunition to Star and Bar to get the place forted up before the Claybury-Gilman bunch brings on its fight!'

They touched spur rowels to their horses and cantered forward along the sun-washed street. Ruth stood back as they moved away, churning dust to the accompaniment of jingling ringbits.

'Take care of yourselves,' she called.

But her eyes were fixed on Rod Strang alone as she spoke.

*   *   *

They rode across the wide, rugged land in thoughtful silence for a long spell.

Strang jogged easily in his saddle, his sombrero yanked over his eyes to ward off the hard glare of the high sun.

He thought of the way this thing was turning out. He'd figured he could hold a lone gun in this region, fighting for the land which he claimed was his. He had known at the start that he was trying to pull wool over his own eyes. No man could stand alone in a range-war and here he was; fighting for Star and Bar, the very outfit he had hated since boyhood. Once, he figured he could start out as a rancher and put his gun-heavy saddle-tramp days behind him — and here he was, riding full tilt into six-gun trouble that might wind up with his corpse being buried in its boots.

He was in the midst of an unfolding pattern which had unfolded elsewhere and which had left bullet-riddled men hugging the earth. It was the pattern Tombstone had seen when the Earp brothers and Doc Holliday marched down Allen Street on an autumn day to meet the Clantons and Sheriff Behan at the OK Corral. It was the pattern Lincoln County had seen when the McSween gunmen came prancing their horses through the New Mexico sunshine to take their part in cutting up a country in a bloody range war. It was a pattern which most men of his kind became involved in sooner or later.

Sooner or later, it brought death. You were only lucky for a certain spell — then you were dead.

Strang thought of his Running S cattle, bought from the savings of hard-scrabble years. Now they were running loose on Star and Bar ground, and he was pushing his nose into Star and Bar's fight. What was the use of trying to work this thing out logically?

What was the use of making plans when the evening might find you dead?

Some miles out of town, in the midst of open country, they came to a sharp drop in the ground, angled their horses down the falling terrain and spotted an abandoned ore wagon lying on its side at the base of the hollow. Both wheels were intact, but the boards of the wagon were warped as though it had lain in the open for a considerable spell.

'What happened there?' asked Strang, nodding towards the wagon as the trio passed it.

'That's a monument to a glorious one-man drinkin' spree,' smiled Warren. 'Old Dutch Gruber who comes in an' out of town for supplies for the Jubilation mine, once brought that old wagon into San Junipero for groceries, but he forgot about the groceries after he got into a lucky monte game in Bannock's saloon. He won himself a tolerable wad an' went a-drinkin' his winnin's. Dutch always claimed he could drive his old ore wagon drunk or sober an' he was so darned drunk that night he had to ask someone to help him into the seat. Well, once he got into the seat, he showed he could drive it drunk, all right. Only trouble was, he drove off in the wrong direction. Instead of headin' for the Jubilation mine, he came out this way to the fringe of Star and Bar land. Then the team blundered down this drop an' the wagon overturned. The team busted loose from the shafts an' strayed. Dutch wasn't hurt an' he was too drunk to care about what had happened. He just lay in the wagon an' slept until mornin', then he walked back to the mine an' the wagon's been here ever since.'

'Never could understand why a man should drink to that extent.' observed Calton with a stony sober face.

Strang and Warren chuckled and the mounted trio topped the rise on the far side of the declivity.

They rode a further mile and they were on Star and Bar grass. A further two miles and they heard a series of stuttering shots which rattled across the wide land from the distance ahead of them. They urged their horses forward and went plunging up a tilted tableland, crested its top and were in good grazing grass. The sharp stammer of shots sounded from the distance continually and, from their high point, the three could see the faraway speck of the Star and Bar ranch house. Even at this distance. they could see riders, dozens of them, it seemed. They were circling the house, riding around the inside of the ranch yard like Indians who had jumped a halted wagon train.

'The Claybury-Gilman gunnies got here first,' said Calton mechanically. 'It looks like they have a whole army down there whoopin' it up!'

Strang snorted and slitted his eyes against the rays of the sun.

'This is their way of retaliatin' for what happened to their gunnies who came into town,' he growled. 'The fellows who got free rode back an' whoever is bossin' this war decided to turn the heat on Star an' Bar while we were still in town.'

'Or else, those rannihans rode into town to fix us while their *amigos* opened up on the ranch,' Warren offered. 'One thing is sure, the Star and Bar crew might be well forted up down there, but we'll have to get to the house pronto with this ammunition. Every slug is goin' to be precious in standin' off that bunch.'

Calton's eyes were fixed on the faraway cameo of bobbing mounted bodies, drifting smoke and furious action from whence came the *pop-pop* of exploding guns which sounded curiously harmless at this distance.

'Ride through that army!' he objected. 'They'd cut us down when we were half-a-mile off!'

'He's right,' Strang told the Marshal quietly. 'If we're goin' to bust in on that fight an' get to the house, we need cover, otherwise, we don't stand a Chinaman's chance.' He suddenly kicked his standing horse into action and hauled its head around to face the direction from which they had come. 'Back this way!' he ordered Warren and Calton urgently. 'I think we can bust in on this fight an' still live long enough to drop a few of those Claybury-Gilman gunnies!'

Orde Clemmins growled an uncomplimentary name in the general direction of the circling Claybury-Gilman raiders who were whirling around the yard of the Star and Bar, fired off the last bullet in his six-shooter then ducked down from the shattered window to thumb shells from his belt loops into the empty chambers of the gun.

'I fought Yankees an' I fought Apaches,' he yelled to Charlie Curry who was close by, levelling a Winchester through the bullet-starred glass of the window. 'But, by the great horny toad, I never figured I'd run across cowmen who descended to Injun tricks of this kind!'

Curry offered no reply save a satisfied grunt following the blast of his carbine which sent a raiding rider pitching into the hoof-mauled dust.

At the windows of the beleaguered Star and Bar headquarters, the hands were making a desperate stand against the raiders who had swept upon them in the full blaze of day. This was the big living room of the house. Furniture had been piled against the doors of the house to make strong barricades and gun-wielding cowpunchers stood at each of the windows blasting shots at the continuously wildly riding Claybury-Gilman gunmen who slammed volleys of shots at the house, shattering windows and tearing at the fabric of the building. Gunsmoke fogged the interior of the house; two Star and Bar hands, old-time Confederates who had once survived the furies of roiling masses of blue and grey, were sprawled in death under a window. Jane Tedrow, showing much of the coolheadedness of her father when in battle, was tying a makeshift bandage around the head of a puncher whose ear had been nicked by a bullet.

From outside, there came the persistent bellow of firearms and the furious yelling of savage men. Jane worked mechanically on the wound of the cowpuncher, trying hard to disguise signs of sinking spirits. It seemed to her, in this desperate stand at the beleaguered headquarters of the ranch that her father had carved out of this rugged land, that the Star and Bar was finished.

These wild men had descended upon the ranch house when they were least expected. A night attack had been expected. The advice of Strang had been taken and the hands had barricaded the house. But the attack had come by day — and the Star and Bar defenders had not had time to lay in an adequate store of ammunition.

And now, the ranch house was under violent attack and a handful of men, mostly the aged veterans of Colonel Tedrow's day, were making a valiant attempt to hold off the Claybury-Gilman gunmen.

But the defenders were running short of ammunition in this wild action in which the Claybury-Gilman riders were trying to scare the Star and Bar men into submission by riding around the house Indian fashion, firing on it from all angles. Jane completed the bandage on the wounded man's head and he snatched up a rifle to take his place at one of the broken windows again. She moved cautiously across the room to the window from which Orde Clemmins and Charlie Curry were pumping shots out into the milling, yelling, shooting bunch of horsemen in the ranch yard. She ducked quickly as an angry bullet tore into the window frame and stripped shards of wood from it.

'How long do you think they'll keep this up?' she asked Clemmins.

'Until they figure we've wasted enough slugs in this hit an' miss shootin', then I guess they'll go to earth an' take us at their leisure,' the foreman answered. 'They jumped us too dad-blamed easy. Someone should have gone to town last night an' got extra shells.'

Charlie Curry nodded assent and the

assent was underlined when he levered the action of his Winchester only to be rewarded with the futile click of an empty magazine.

'Darned thing is empty.' growled Curry in disgust, 'an' I bet every last shell in the place has been used up — ' He stopped in mid-sentence, his eyes fixed unbelievingly on something out beyond the dust and smoke hazed welter of charging riders passing the window.

This window was at the front of the house, facing the entrance to the ranch yard with its high arched gate from which swung a shingle branded with the Star and Bar iron which Cal Tedrow had devised from the old Rebel flag. Framed in that gate, growing bigger in a billowing banner of dust and coming directly for the Star and Bar headquarters, was a fast moving wagon. From this distance, it looked like a heavy ore wagon such as those used at the mineral mines. It was hauled by three horses and whoever rode in it was keeping well down below the high, iron-bound wooden sides.

'What do you make of this?' yelled Curry.

Crouching low, Curry, Clemmins and Jane Tedrow watched the approaching wagon in dumbfounded silence. Whoever gripped the reins inside that high-walled wagon was flicking them madly across the backs of the team of three and his hoarse yells as he urged the animals onward could be heard even at this distance. The whirling Claybury-Gilman riders saw the ore wagon trundling for the gate of the yard at its furious rate. One of them halted his horse and triggered a panicky shot at the wagon. Immediately, a man's head appeared briefly over the side of the approaching wagon. The sun flashed a brief sheen on the six-shooter in his hand, then the rider who had fired was diving down out of his saddle making clutching movements at his chest. A second head appeared over the side of the wagon, a second gun blasted and a second raiding horseman was slumping in his saddle.

Then the three horses and the wagon were at the gate, rolling through it into the thick of the marauding riders.

Jane Tedrow. Charlie Curry and Orde Clemmins watched it approach with a wide-eyed and petrified fascination. They now knew who was entering this fight in this novel manner.

For the first head which had emerged over the top of the heavily protected wagon was that of San Junipero's one-armed marshal. And the second was that of Rod Strang.

14

Crouching low in the heavily trundling ore wagon, George Calton gripped the leathers and yelled hoarsely, urging forward the three horses, divested of their saddles and hastily accommodated between the warped shafts of the wagon drunken Dutch Gruber had left out on the range. Animals plunged wild-eyed and snorting into the roiling midst of the bullet-banquet which was under way in the ranch yard of the Star and Bar. Bullets whanged through the curling wreaths of gunsmoke and clipped shards off the weathered boards of the wagon.

Strang and Warren, one on either side of the wagon, triggered shots at the Claybury-Gilman raiders. Marauders dropped from their saddles as the heavy wagon came rolling like a horse-drawn, fire-spitting tornado through the arched gate of the yard, others wheeled their animals about and made an attempt to answer the slamming six-guns flourished by the pair in the wagon. Others still, realized that they were caught between two sets of fire: one from the defenders in the ranch house and the other issuing from the madly careering ore wagon. They spurred their horses out of their dangerous position hastily and holed up by the fence rails surrounding the yard.

The yard was a crackling chaos of floundering horses; dead and wounded men sprawled in the mauled dust and others took advantage of the cover offered by the humped carcasses of horses or the stout posts of the peeled pole fence in order to fire on the house and the newcomers. Strang and Warren pumped shots through the fog of powdersmoke and, as the wagon came into the thick of the mêlée in the yard, George Calton loosed the reins and grabbed up his Winchester from the floor of the trundling vehicle. He added its throaty roar to the angry sound of the battle.

The arrival of the trio in the ore wagon had broken the Claybury-Gilman faction's tactic of continually circling the ranch house. The raiders were now mostly dismounted and holed-up, trying desperately to cancel out this new factor of three bullet-throwing men in a crazily rocking and swaying wagon, hauled by a team of near-crazed horses. But the wagon continued to roll across the wide yard. its occupants well protected by the high, iron-bound walls over the top of which they made frequent appearances to slash the hazing gunsmoke with accurately aimed shots. The three horses plunged and lurched onward, heading directly towards the veranda of the house.

Jane Tedrow, Orde Clemmins, Charlie Curry and half-a-dozen of the Star and Bar hands were congregated at a shattered window watching the wagon's approach and pitching shots at the now disorganized Claybury-Gilman riders.

'That blamed old wagon is plumb out of control?' exclaimed Curry. 'It's bound to hit the veranda, the cayuses are crazy with all this shootin'!'

The girl and the cowpokes at the window watched Charlie Curry's words come true, the incident being acted out with a strange semblance of slow motion. Jane stifled a scream as the three madly lunging horses thudded against the veranda rail close to the main steps. With a sharp snap, the shafts, made rotten by months of lying in the open, shattered and the horses were snorting, kicking and mauling themselves free. At the same time, the wagon appeared to be turning slowly and easily over on its side while Rod Strang, Dan Warren and George Calton were rolling out of it in a threshing tangle of arms and legs.

The Claybury-Gilman riders, holed up at their various points of the yard, began to slam shots in their direction. Leaden hornets were zipping angrily through the acrid fog. One dropped a struggling horse between the shafts, others thudded into the thick boards or sang spitefully off the iron-rimmed wheels.

'Cover 'em!' bellowed Orde Clemmins. He shoved Jane Tedrow away from the window, hefted his six-shooter through the starred glass and blasted out a fusillade of shots in the direction of a clutter of raiders who were firing from cover against the fence. His companions at the window joined him in sending a withering stream of fire across the yard, giving Strang, Warren and Calton an opportunity to recover their weapons and establish themselves behind the overturned wagon. Warren slithered into the shelter of the wagon, leaned against its now vertical floor and gripped his pistol between his knees while he shoved shells into its empty chambers.

With a curiously whimsical expression, the one-armed marshal had his lips pursed and whistled the old cavalry tune 'Garryowen' as hostile bullets hummed around him.

Rod Strang lost a tooth in the fall from the wagon. He jetted a red stream into the dust as he crawled into the cover of the wagon. He remembered the way Warren had fought him in the street back in town and remembered the legends they told about the way he got his men out of the Dragoons when he was seriously wounded in Geronimo's attack. For the second time that day, he was glad Warren was fighting on his side.

'You blamed hellion, Warren,' he growled good-naturedly, 'I declare you thrive on fightin'.'

'Keeps a man from goin' blue mouldy,' declared Warren laconically as he squirmed flat on his stomach to fire around the side of the wagon. George Calton was already sprawled spread-legged in the lee of the wagon, sending lances of muzzle-fire and red hot bullets through the curling cordite wreaths with his Winchester.

Strang joined him, triggering his Colt at the main pocket of holed-up resistance until there was a sudden lull in the fighting. Away beyond the fence-rail, he saw a flurry of riding men, half-a-dozen of them, riding away from the ranch.

'Some of 'em are cuttin' an' runnin',' he yelled to Warren. 'They've had enough!' He turned his head to see that Warren was moving away from the wagon. He had holstered his gun and clutched the gunny sack of ammunition in his hand. Moving at a crouch, he was negotiating the tangle of shattered wagon shafts in order to reach the steps of the veranda and pass the ammunition to Clemmins and the rest of the Star and Bar cowhands framed in the window.

Strang and Calton saw the danger in his move and yelled a warning together. There was still much active opposition from the raiders who were bunched together over by the fence rails, and they were in a position to sweep the veranda with fire.

Even as Warren stepped free of the broken shafts, the first crackle of fire sounded from the raiders over by the fence.

'They'll kill him for sure,' complained Calton as he prepared to answer the firing. 'Just look at the madman. He's tryin' to get to that window, but he'll never make it!'

Warren was going through with it determinedly. Crouching and moving swiftly, he was travelling along the veranda which was wide open to the raiders. He had a run of several yards before him to make it to the window with the sack of ammunition and bullets were already spanging around him.

Strang joined Calton in slinging slugs across the yard. As he fired, he attempted to watch Warren's progress from the corner of his eye.

'The dad-blamed fool,' he grunted savagely. 'This time, he's askin' to be killed!' The six-shooter bucked and thundered in his fist until its chambers were empty then as he slithered into the lee of the wagon to recharge the weapon, he saw Warren stagger the last yard to the window.

'He's hit!' croaked Calton. 'They've hit him for sure!'

Jane Tedrow's shrill scream was heard from inside the house, but the marshal was still on his feet. With what seemed to be a supreme effort, he passed the heavy sack to the grasping hands protruding from the window. Then he pitched forward on his face and rolled across the bullet-bitten veranda to rest against its railing and remain there completely still.

A crimson rage welled up in Rod Strang. The hired border scum of cowardly range-hogs had killed a man of cool, tough cavalry courage. There seemed to be an element of injustice in its occurring right at this moment when the raiders were beginning to show signs of weakening and some had already hazed for the distance.

A searing flame of anger burned in Strang. Nothing seemed to matter to him now other than evening up for the death of Dan Warren. He'd do it, by thunder, just as he found the man who had shot Nacio from ambush. A curious cold logic began to work inside his skull despite the flaring anger he felt.

He saw that, in the final analysis, the men responsible for Warren's death were those responsible for that of Nacio; Claybury and Gilman, the bosses of the Chicago cattle combine that paid gunsharps such as Lafe Alford and lesser border ruffians to brawl across other people's land. Somehow, he thought savagely, he would even the score for both Nacio and Dan Warren, even it with the top men of the Claybury-Gilman combine!

From behind the wagon. Strang and Calton pumped slugs across the yard. A crackling fury of gunfire from the house backed their gunsong as the defenders made use of the ammunition Warren had passed to them.

A last furious pattern of action unfolded in the ranch yard with Strang and Calton triggering shots at the remaining raiders and a stuttering fusillade pounded from the windows of the house. Then, the opposition was breaking. More raiders were hazing for the wide yonder and others were searching for horses on which to follow them. Suddenly, Strang caught sight of a familiar face among the wildly running raiders.

An irresistible fury possessed Strang. He put up his gun and went charging out of the cover of the overturned wagon, haring through mists of gunsmoke in the direction of the owner of the familiar face. The man was panicky, running for a loose horse which he hoped to mount. He turned his head, saw Strang coming behind him and put on a spurt of speed. But Strang lengthened his stride then gave a flying leap through the air to grip the fugitive by

230

the shoulders and haul him backwards.

The man protested and struggled. He was a small, sandy haired and foxy faced man, one who had already seen enough of Rod Strang and who wanted only to ride for a change of scenery in company with his fellow ruffians who had sold their guns into this range-war which had come apart at the seams.

Strang bunched a fist under the sandy one's nose.

'Who's bossing this land grab?' he demanded.

'Quit maulin' me,' complained the captive.

'I'll maul you until you see stars,' threatened Strang. 'Tell me who's bossin' this ruckus. Claybury an' Gilman don't come in fightin' themselves, but they hire some hellion to act as their general in the field. Now you tell me who's ramroddin' this particular fight.'

'Mitch Petersen,' whimpered the sandy one. 'Lay off me, will you? I want to get out of here. I should have got out before like the kid did, he took off after he got his busted leg in a splint. Said this thing had started badly for him an' he'd rather ride yonderly with a busted leg than stay in the fight an' get killed.'

'He acted wisely,' Strang growled. 'You should have joined him. But you didn't, so you'll answer my questions. You mean Mitch Petersen from the Indian Territory is bossin' this thing for the Claybury-Gilman outfit?'

'Yeah, the same one. There's only one Petersen,' answered the foxy faced man. 'An' he's a darn sight faster than Lafe Alford!'

This last observation appeared to be in the nature of a warning to Strang, but he paid no attention to it.

'He kept well clear of the fight, didn't he?'

'Sure, he was paid to ramrod it, not get himself killed.'

'An' he prodded this whole thing? He sent that bunch of rannihans into town to mix it with the marshal an' me while the rest of you swooped down here on Star an' Bar?'

'Sure, he gave orders for the whole thing. But you prodded it along — this thing wasn't planned that way, but when you jumped Lafe an' the kid an' me at the linecamp you prodded Mitch into action.'

'Yeah, I understand,' Strang murmured. 'You originally planned to play it slow an' easy with dodges like cuttin' off Star and Bar water an' maybe runnin' off some stock or burnin' some pastures. Where is Petersen now?'

'He hazed for the distance when you an' that marshal began bustin' this raid open. That was when the rest of us got squeamish. Ain't no point in the troops stayin' in the field when the general runs for it.'

'There ain't,' affirmed Strang cynically. 'So Mitch got yellow an' so did the rest of you. Where d'you figure he headed for?'

'Tombstone, I guess.'

'Tombstone? Why Tombstone?'

'Claybury and Gilman are there. They owe Petersen money for his part in the fight. He said he was clearin' out of here for Tombstone to collect what they owe him.'

Rod shoved the foxy faced man away from him.

'Clear out of here an' don't let me cross trails with you again, *hombre*,' he advised.

Thoughts of vengeance surged in his mind. So Claybury and Gilman, the powers behind this range war, were in Tombstone, doubtless watching this attempted land-grab from a distance. The story that Amos Gilman had left for Chicago was untrue — he had travelled to a point no further than Tombstone and there had met his partner Claybury. Maybe, if he pushed his luck, he could even up with them — even up for Nacio, for Dan Warren and for the brothers Walker and their cowhands who had come to grief in the earlier Claybury-Gilman landgrab far from here.

He turned and wandered through the thinning palls of gunsmoke shrouding the ranch yard littered with the debris of war, looking for a horse fit to ride to Tombstone. On the veranda of the ranch house, he saw Jane Tedrow, George Calton and a band of Star and Bar hands. Someone waved to him and shouted something which he couldn't hear. He found a sturdy little paint pony, saddled and wandering about the now silent yard without a rider.

Strang climbed into the saddle and rode off the Star and Bar headquarters, once more a man with a lonesome gun.

15

It was dark when Strang reached Tombstone. Stars sparkled in the night-filled vault of the sky over that rowdy town. Allen Street was astir with miners and cowhands: the wavering notes of a singing dance hall girl were heard from the Oriental Saloon and a squeaky orchestra was playing in the Birdcage Theatre. At the corner of Allen and First Street, a couple of drunken miners were having a fist-fight and a wobbly-legged cowboy staggered out of the Crystal Palace to fall flat on his face in the dust as he tried to step off the sidewalk.

Tombstone, the rip-roaring town that got started almost by accident where Ed Schieffelin struck silver in '77, was warming up for the night!

Rod Strang rode in wearily, sitting his saddle like a man in a half-dream. He headed the paint's nose along the wide vista of Allen Street where dozens of oil-lamps splashed their glow across the sidewalks and rutted street surface from saloons and stores. Somewhere in this town were Claybury and Gilman and somewhere was Mitch Petersen. Strang was determined to seek them out. He was a lonesome man with a lone gun, on the vengeance trail for his Mexican partner, for a devil-may-care cavalryman turned marshal and for the Walker Brothers and their butchered South Dakota cowpokes. Claybury and Gilman would be easy to handle, they were city slickers with blood on their hands, but not fighting men. Strang figured he could deal out rough frontier justice in their case.

Mitch Petersen was different. He was a challenge.

Petersen represented a species which had now largely had its day: the professional gunslinger of the trail-towns. Just as the days of Abilene. Witchita and Dodge had faded, most of his kind had faded from the scene, many of them violently. Wild Bill Hickok had been shot through the head in a card game in Deadwood; Ben Thompson, who had rampaged around the wide-open trail towns in the days of the cattle drives, had returned to his native Texas to be gunned down in a San Antonio saloon and Wyatt Earp, in company with his bullet-throwing dentist friend Doc Holliday, had hit a smart lick out of this very Tombstone after the OK Corral fight to pursue another line of life.

Others had lived through their brief hour of bullet-bitten glory to die with their boots on, but Mitch Petersen from the Indian Territory was still alive. He was a fast gunhand and a vicious killer, but Strang knew he would have to be faced.

He was well known. If he was in Tombstone, he would not require much finding.

Strang dismounted outside a small saloon, hitched his horse and went inside. He elbowed his way to the bar and ordered a whiskey. A scrubby bearded barmar served him.

'I heard Mitch Petersen is in town,' stated Strang. 'Know where I can find him?'

A hush fell on the men crowding the bar. Glasses were stilled on their way to lips. Eyes turned to Strang's thonged down holster.

The barkeep nodded towards the door.

'I heard he was last seen goin' into Mifflin's Hotel, just across the street,' he said quietly.

Strang nodded his thanks, downed his drink and walked out.

★   ★   ★

Mifflin's Hotel was a small establishment which kept up a show of citified sophistication. Strang walked off the street into a small vestibule which had faded plush seats and potted palms. A fat man in a frock-coat was leaning against the reception desk behind which lolled a stringy-necked clerk who wore steel-rimmed glasses.

The eyes of this pair were riveted on the dusty, weary-faced man who strode purposefully in with a Colt strung down to his thigh.

The fat man asked: 'What can I do for you?'

'You can tell me if Mitch Petersen is in here!'

The fat man's eyebrows lifted in alarm and his eyes flew to the tied-down holster sported by Strang.

'Now, we don't want any shooting in here,' he said in jittery spurts. 'This place is respectable!'

'I have no time for conversation,' said Strang tartly. 'Tell me where he is.'

'Room four, that's four doors along the corridor at the top of the stairs,' the fat man said, capitulating before Strang's determined manner. 'He's in there with two gentlemen from Chicago.'

'Mr Claybury and Mr Gilman,' smiled Strang. 'I have business with all three of them. You two better follow me up the stairs and keep well behind me — I want a couple of witnesses.'

The pair began to protest vigorously.

'You can't burst in here an' cause trouble,' spluttered the fat man. 'I own this hotel and I keep a respectable place.'

'I told you I have no time for conversation,' repeated Strang. 'Get behind me an' be ready to duck.'

They followed him sheepishly up the steeply inclined stairs. Strang catfooted along the corridor to the door marked '4'.

He could hear voices from beyond the door. An argument about money appeared to be in progress and he guessed that Claybury and Gilman were holding back Mitch Petersen's money because the grab for Star and Bar land had been badly botched. Strang grasped the handle and thrust the door open; the owner of the hotel and his clerk ducked out of the direct line of fire from the room.

Strang stood framed in the doorway.

Facing him were Claybury, Gilman and Petersen, making a tableau around a table. Gilman, with his elegant side-whiskers, sat at one side of the table. Claybury, a heavily built man with sharp features, was sitting across from him. Petersen was standing behind the table, facing the door. He was tall and lean with a sweeping longhorn moustache. He wore the broadcloth suit of a gambling man and his coat was hitched back to reveal a Colt .45 slung low at his hip. His face was totally unsurprised, he looked a man who had never been surprised in his life, but the Chicago men sat petrified in their chairs, round eyes staring at the dusty, gun-packing apparition which had shown up at the door.

'I've come to settle a few scores,' Rod said calmly. 'Scores for Star and Bar, scores for the Walkin' W an' a score for my partner who was shot on your orders because we looked like buttin' in where we were not wanted. The gunnie who shot him would have shot me, too, but I scared him out of his hidin' hole.' The words were meant for Claybury and Gilman, but Strang did not remove his eyes from Mitch Petersen's face as he spoke them. 'I think,' he added easily, 'we ought to get to shootin'.'

Petersen chuckled lightly.

'You're talkin' too big, young feller, I'm Mitch Petersen.'

'I know it, an' you're gettin' old. There's always a younger an' faster *hombre* comin' up on the heels of yore kind.'

The owner of Mifflin's Hotel and his clerk felt chills creeping up their spines. They were listening to this dusty stranger prodding the notorious Mitch Petersen into a gunfight. Out on the street, Tombstone was rowdy but the din seemed to be a million miles away, a tiny stirring of noise behind the climbing tension as these two faced each other across the hotel room.

Petersen chuckled again and said, with the tone of one engaged in friendly conversation: 'You surely don't think you're the young *hombre* who's faster than me?' Then he drew his revolver with eye-baffling speed. But the younger man's gun was out of leather and in his fist a fraction of a second earlier. It flared out a blossom of fire and its bellow was deafening in the tiny room.

Mitch Petersen did not even trigger his Colt. It was still cold in his hand as he crumpled down in a slack heap, like a marionette all of whose strings had suddenly been cut.

Claybury and Gilman had not shifted their petrified bodies from the surprised pose they held at the table. The hotel owner and the clerk shoved their faces cautiously around the door.

'I guess you can testify that this was a stand up man-to-man affair, if you're ever called on to do so,' Strang told them. He nodded to the clerk. 'Bring some paper an' a pen, these gentlemen are goin' to do a little writin'.'

As the clerk scuttled away, Strang holstered his gun and jerked his head towards the crumpled body of Mitch Petersen.

'He can't help you any more,' he told Claybury and Gilman. 'You have no hired gunmen around you now an' you're plumb finished.'

When the clerk returned with the paper and writing materials, Strang made Claybury write a statement and made both sign it. He told the hotel proprietor and the clerk to add their signatures as witnesses. Then he appended his own name under a note that he could vouch for the statements written by the Chicago cattle magnates.

It was a document of value, declaring that the Claybury-Gilman combine had recruited gunmen to steal cattlelands in remote regions and had connived at murder.

Strang folded it and slid it into his shirt pocket.

'This is goin' to find its way to Washington,' he said. 'It means that you two have signed yoreselves out of yore graspin' murderin' business. What you do now is no concern of mine. You can hang around on United States territory until you're finally arrested, or you can run over the border to Mexico.' He turned to the proprietor and the clerk and said: 'Thanks for yore help. How much do I pay for a wash an' shave an' a room where I might sleep for three or four hours?'

* * *

It was close to midday the following day when Strang reached the Star and Bar ranch house. He had slept well at the Tombstone hotel and he prodded the paint pony across Star and Bar lands with his spirits poised between elation and depression. The Claybury-Gilman outfit was broken, which was a matter for elation, but the depression was brought on by his reflections on the way his own personal fight had gone.

He came into this region with a partner and now his partner was gone. He came to fight a range tyrant and found the old order had changed and that Cal Tedrow was not, after all, quite the ogre he had imagined in his youth. He came here with cattle, but Tedrow's daughter, with her tough fighting spirit, had cut them loose to wander her ranges.

His fortunes had turned full circle and he was once more a lone man with a lonesome gun. A gun which had achieved something for others in this desert-edge rangeland — but precious little for himself.

What, he thought again, was the use of making plans?

He reached the Star and Bar house with the intention of saying his farewells, but the door burst open and Jane Tedrow was suddenly on the veranda with Ruth Calton following her and several of the Star and Bar riders. There was an unfathomable joyfulness in their attitude.

'You're back!' exclaimed Jane. 'Where have you been?'

'Tombstone, to finish this out. It's all finished. The Claybury-Gilman combine will make no more land grabs.'

They hustled him into the house and, on the threshold of the big living room, he stopped in his tracks. George Calton was standing there — and with him was Marshal Dan Warren with a turban-like bandage covering his head. Strang goggled at the one-armed marshal.

'I thought you were dead!' he managed to say.

'Knocked cold by a bullet is all,' commented Warren. 'It sort of side-swiped me on the temple just as I passed the ammunition to the boys in the house!'

Strang sat down in a chair heavily. 'Well, doggone!' he murmured. 'I thought you were dead!'

'We tried to tell you he wasn't, but you were too busy catchin' that horse,' explained George Calton and Rod remembered the way the knot of people on the veranda had called something to him as he was about to ride away.

Ruth Calton was suddenly before him, smiling.

'Anything to eat?' she asked. 'Coffee

and flapjacks, for instance.'

'Coffee and flapjacks will be fine,' he responded, then enquired: 'What are you doin' here?'

'I came out when I heard about the battle that went on here. I thought I might be able to bandage wounds and cook meals.'

'And a very welcome addition to the household you are,' laughed Jane Tedrow. 'There's going to be a heap of cooking required around here in the next few days. A bunch of men are starting out on a round-up.'

'A round-up?' queried Rod blankly.

'Cutting out Running S beef from Star and Bar beef, so you can start out ranching on your land. My boys will help you build your house,' explained Jane.

Strang stared at her dully.

'That land is going to be yours,' Cal Tedrow's daughter went on 'Forget the old squabble about who has a right to it, we're agreeing here and now that it's yours. There's no need to go bickering and fighting about it, there's been enough of that in this country.'

'An' if there's ever any help or advice needed, don't forget to consult me. Ain't much about cattle raisin' I don't know,' piped up George Calton.

Strang settled back in his chair. 'Now take it easy. Things aren't the same as they were when I rode into this country. I had a good partner then an' now he's dead. A man needs a partner in a venture like startin' out as a rancher.'

'A partner or a good wife,' put in Dan Warren wisely.

Ruth Calton brought in the flapjacks and coffee and she smiled at Strang.

'Done the way you like them.' she commented.

'Yeah,' mused Rod, half-aloud. 'A partner or a good wife.' It suddenly seemed to him that there was a whole lot of sense in making plans. He returned Ruth's smile and said to the company in general:

'Okay. When do we start the round-up?'